ON the CASE with HOLMES and WATSON

SHERLOCK HOLMES

and the Adventure at the Copper Beeches

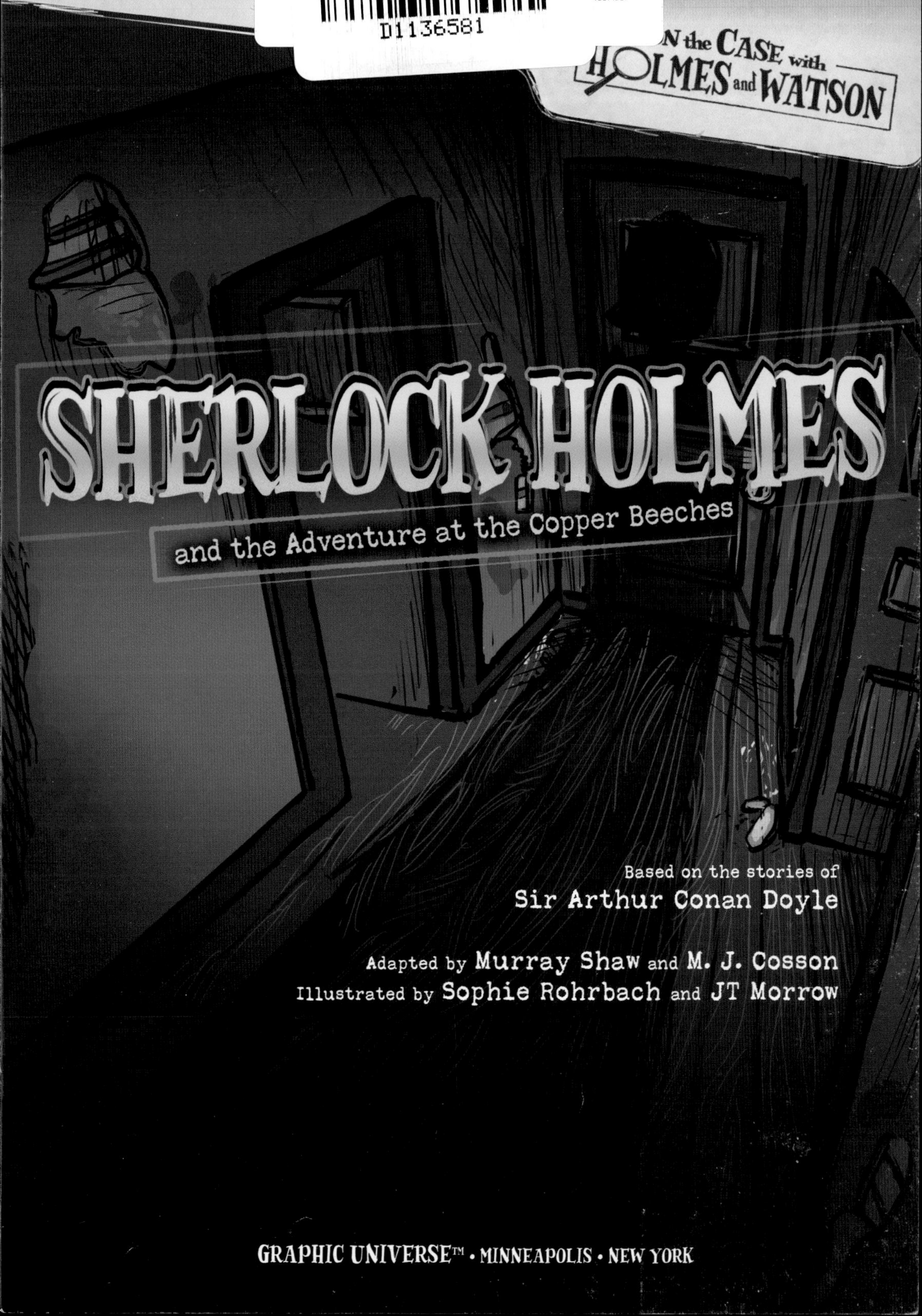

Based on the stories of
Sir Arthur Conan Doyle

Adapted by Murray Shaw and M. J. Cosson
Illustrated by Sophie Rohrbach and JT Morrow

GRAPHIC UNIVERSE™ • MINNEAPOLIS • NEW YORK

Grateful acknowledgment to Dame Jean Conan Doyle for permission to use the
Sherlock Holmes characters created by Sir Arthur Conan Doyle

Text copyright © 2012 by Murray Shaw
Illustrations © 2012 by Lerner Publishing Group, Inc.

Graphic Universe™ is a trademark of Lerner Publishing Group, Inc.

Graphic Universe™
A division of Lerner Publishing Group, Inc.
241 First Avenue North
Minneapolis, MN 55401 U.S.A.

Website address: www.lernerbooks.com

Library of Congress Cataloging-in-Publication Data

Shaw, Murray.
    Sherlock Holmes and the adventure at the Copper Beeches / adapted by
Murray Shaw and M.J. Cosson ; illustrated by Sophie Rohrbach and JT Morrow
; from the original stories by Sir Arthur Conan Doyle.
        p.   cm. — (On the case with Holmes and Watson ; #08)
    Summary: Retold in graphic novel form, Sherlock Holmes investigates if
there is danger afoot when a young woman is asked to cut off her long hair
and dress in a specific blue gown in order to be hired as governess at the
Copper Beeches. Includes a section explaining Holmes's reasoning and the
clues he used to solve the mystery.
        ISBN: 978-0-7613-7087-1 (lib. bdg. : alk. paper)
        I. Graphic novels. (I. Graphic novels. 2. Doyle, Arthur Conan, Sir,
1859–1930. Adventure of the Copper Beeches—Adaptations. 3. Mystery and
detective stories.) I. Cosson, M. J. II. Rohrbach, Sophie, ill. III. Morrow,
JT, ill. IV. Doyle, Arthur Conan, Sir, 1859–1930. Adventure of the Copper
Beeches. V. Title. VI. Title: Adventure at the Copper Beeches.
    PZ7.7.S46Shh 2011   2010031982
    741.5'973—dc22

Manufactured in the United States of America
1—BC—7/15/11

The Story of
SHERLOCK HOLMES
the Famous Detective

Sherlock Holmes and his helpful friend Dr. John Watson are fictional characters created by British writer Sir Arthur Conan Doyle. Doyle published his first novel about the pair, *A Study in Scarlet*, in 1887, and it became very successful. Doyle went on to write fifty-six short stories, as well as three more novels about Holmes's adventures—*The Sign of Four* (1890), *The Hound of the Baskervilles* (1902), and *The Valley of Fear* (1915).

Sherlock Holmes and Dr. Watson have become some of the most famous book characters of all time. Holmes spent most of his time solving mysteries, but he also had a wide array of hobbies, such as playing the violin, boxing, and sword fighting. Watson, a retired army doctor, met Holmes through a mutual friend when Holmes was looking for a roommate. Watson lived with Holmes for several years at 221B Baker Street before marrying and moving out. However, after his marriage, Watson continued to assist Holmes with his cases.

The original versions of the Sherlock Holmes stories are still printed, and many have been made into movies and television shows. Readers continue to be impressed by Holmes's detective methods of observation and scientific reason.

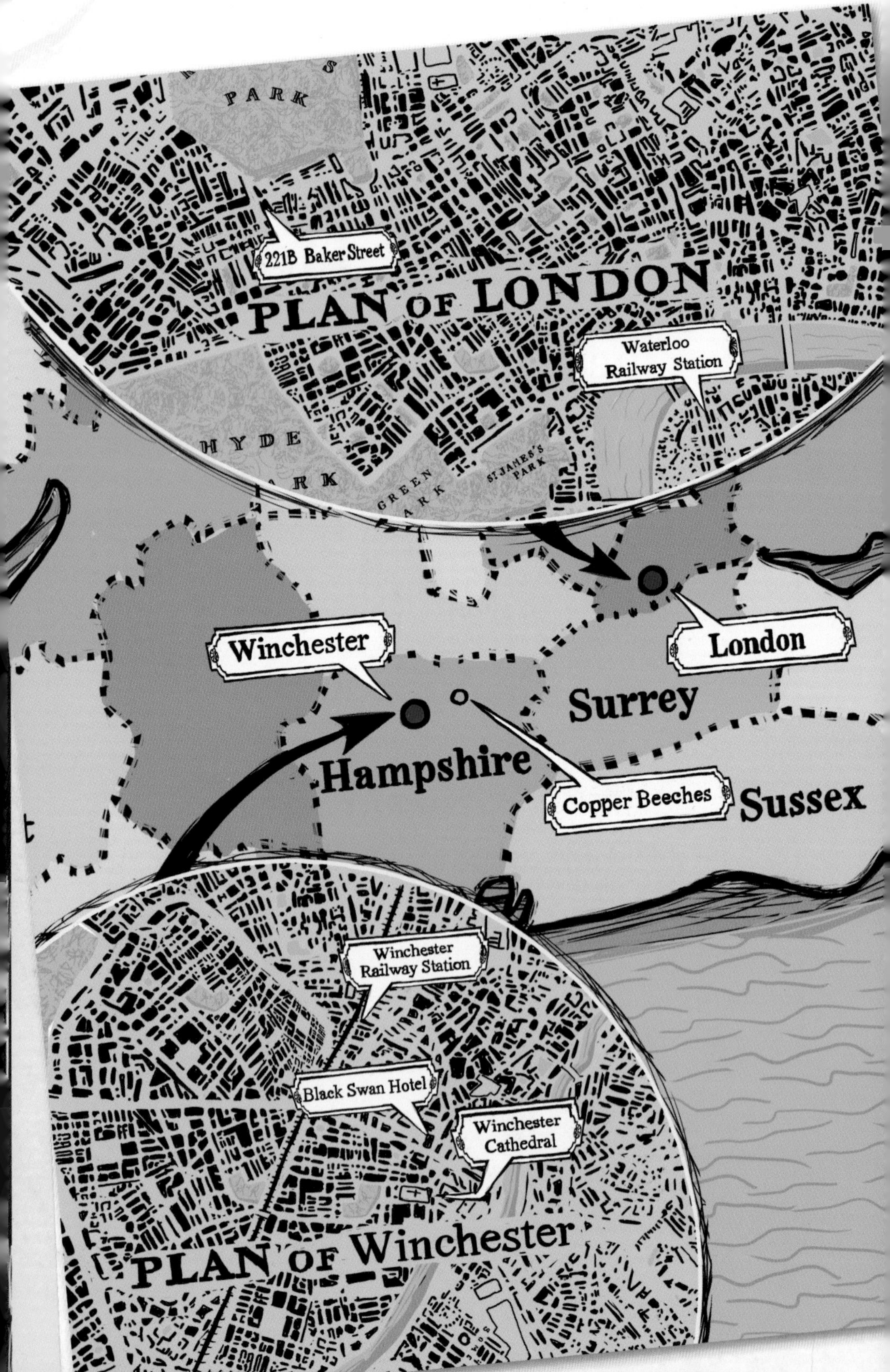
PARK
221B Baker Street
PLAN OF LONDON
Waterloo Railway Station
HYDE PARK
GREEN PARK
ST JAMES'S PARK
London
Winchester
Surrey
Hampshire
Copper Beeches
Sussex
Winchester Railway Station
Black Swan Hotel
Winchester Cathedral
PLAN OF Winchester

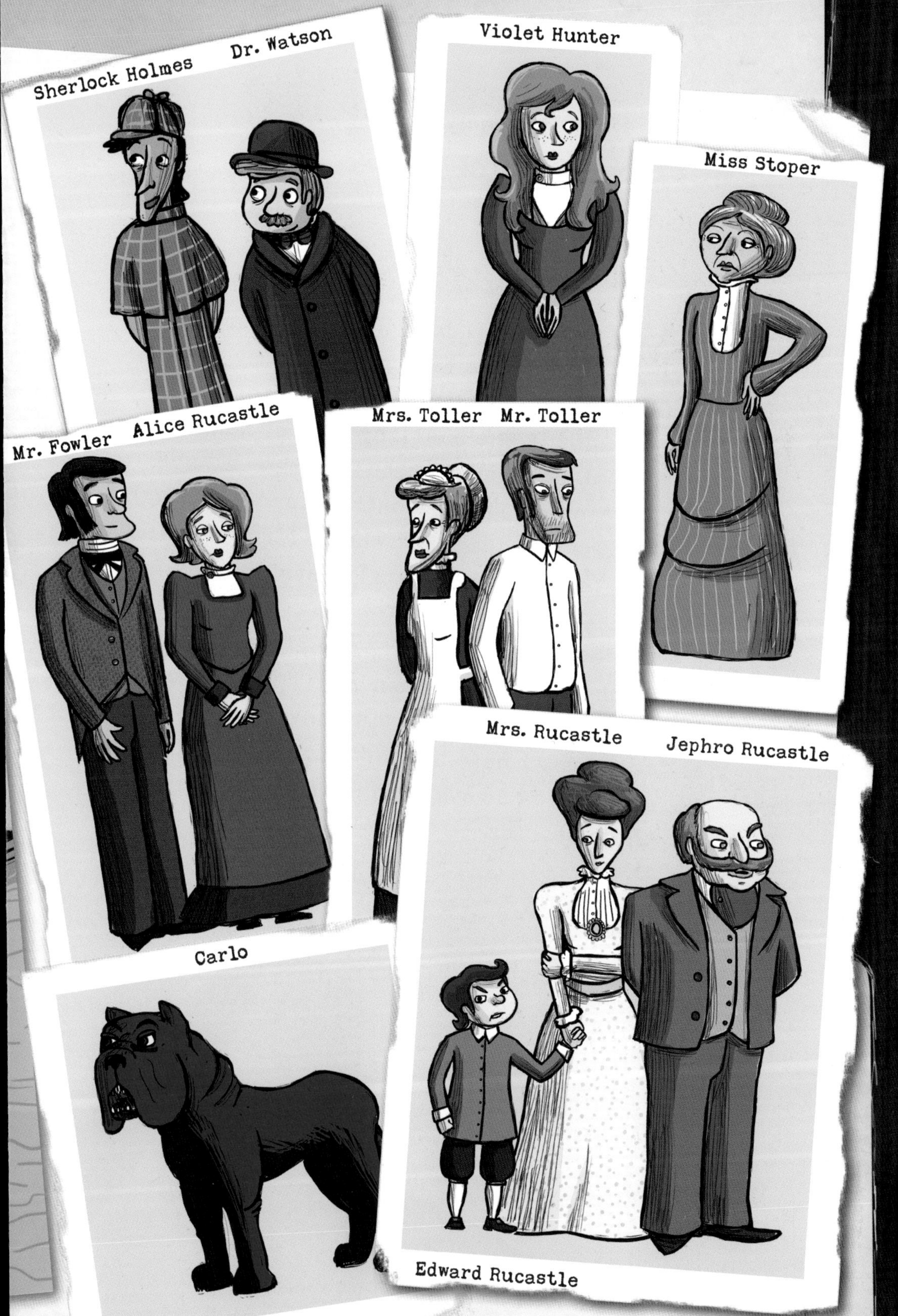
Sherlock Holmes
Dr. Watson
Violet Hunter
Miss Stoper
Mr. Fowler
Alice Rucastle
Mrs. Toller
Mr. Toller
Mrs. Rucastle
Jephro Rucastle
Carlo
Edward Rucastle

From the Desk of
John H. Watson, M.D.

My name is Dr. John H. Watson. For several years, I have been assisting my friend, Sherlock Holmes, in solving mysteries throughout the bustling city of London and beyond. Holmes is a peculiar man—always questioning and reasoning his way through various problems. But when I first met him in 1878, I was immediately intrigued by his oddities.

Holmes has always been more daring than I, and his logical deduction never ceases to amaze me. I have begun writing down all of the adventures I have with Holmes. This is one of those stories.

Sincerely,

Dr. Watson

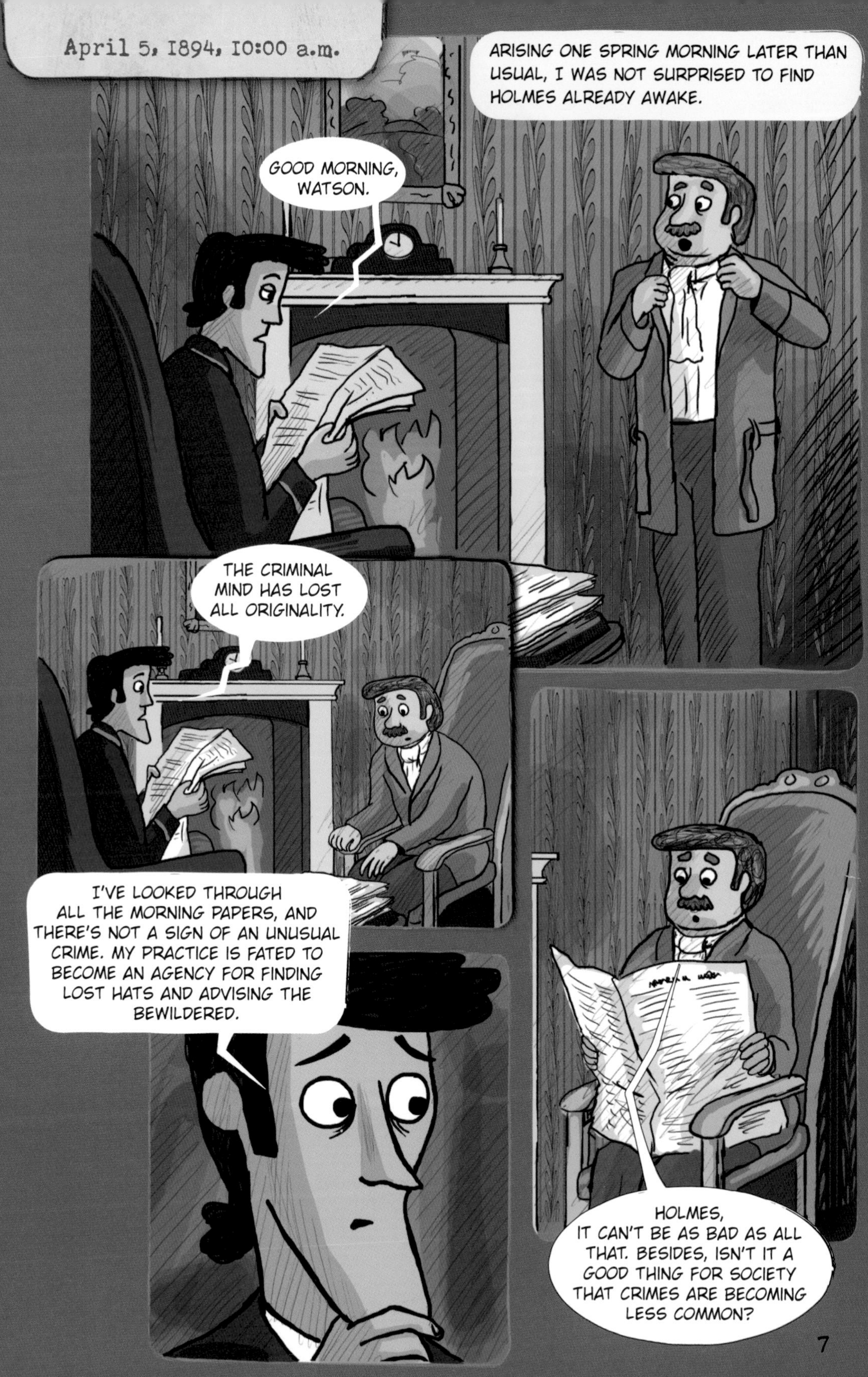

April 5, 1894, 10:00 a.m.
ARISING ONE SPRING MORNING LATER THAN USUAL, I WAS NOT SURPRISED TO FIND HOLMES ALREADY AWAKE.
GOOD MORNING, WATSON.
THE CRIMINAL MIND HAS LOST ALL ORIGINALITY.
I'VE LOOKED THROUGH ALL THE MORNING PAPERS, AND THERE'S NOT A SIGN OF AN UNUSUAL CRIME. MY PRACTICE IS FATED TO BECOME AN AGENCY FOR FINDING LOST HATS AND ADVISING THE BEWILDERED.
HOLMES, IT CAN'T BE AS BAD AS ALL THAT. BESIDES, ISN'T IT A GOOD THING FOR SOCIETY THAT CRIMES ARE BECOMING LESS COMMON?

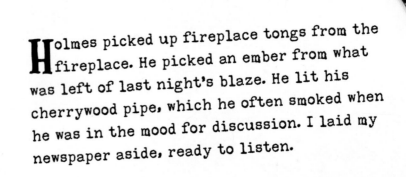

Holmes picked up fireplace tongs from the fireplace. He picked an ember from what was left of last night's blaze. He lit his cherrywood pipe, which he often smoked when he was in the mood for discussion. I laid my newspaper aside, ready to listen.

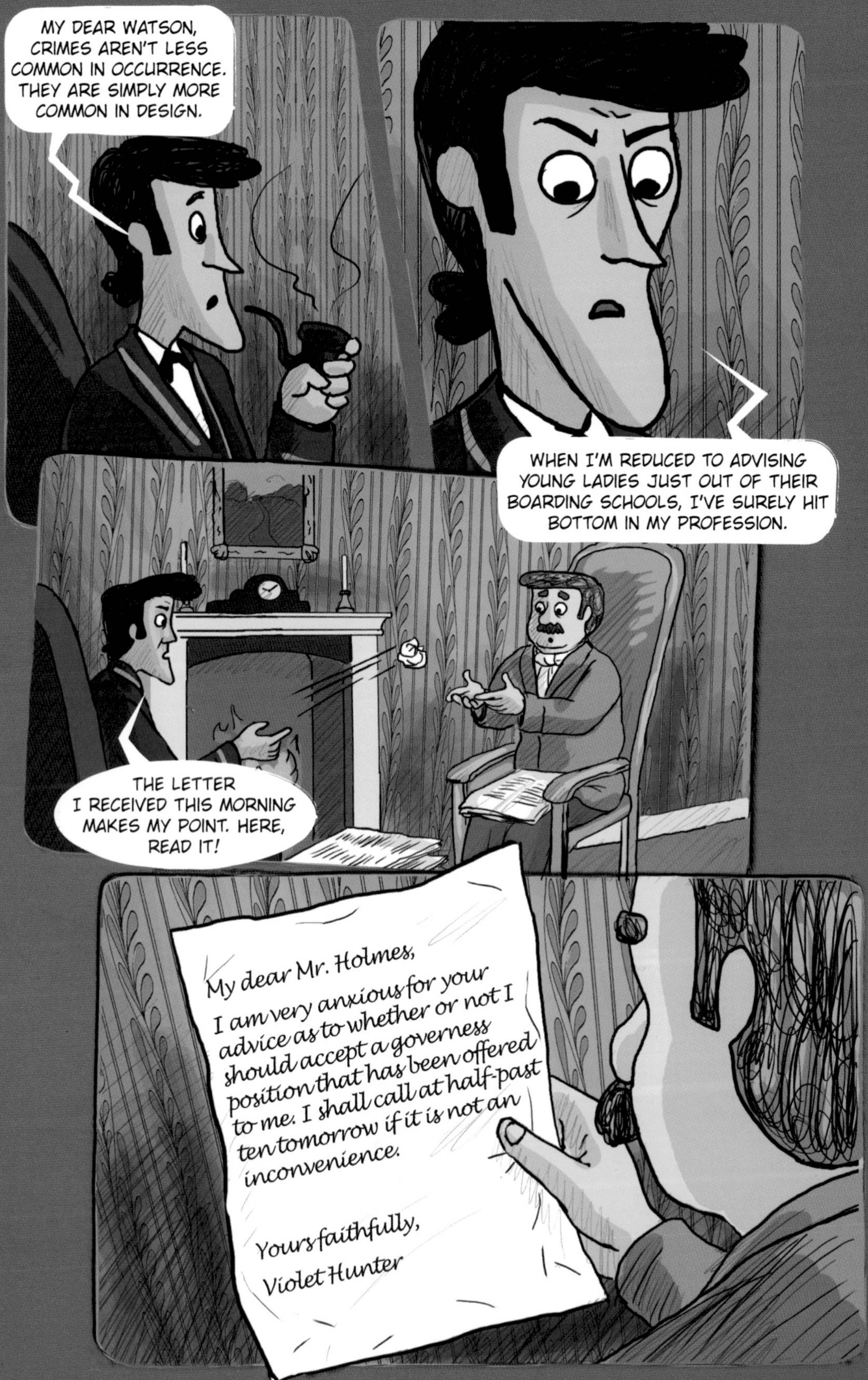
MY DEAR WATSON, CRIMES AREN'T LESS COMMON IN OCCURRENCE. THEY ARE SIMPLY MORE COMMON IN DESIGN.
WHEN I'M REDUCED TO ADVISING YOUNG LADIES JUST OUT OF THEIR BOARDING SCHOOLS, I'VE SURELY HIT BOTTOM IN MY PROFESSION.
THE LETTER I RECEIVED THIS MORNING MAKES MY POINT. HERE, READ IT!
My dear Mr. Holmes,
I am very anxious for your advice as to whether or not I should accept a governess position that has been offered to me. I shall call at half-past ten tomorrow if it is not an inconvenience.
Yours faithfully,
Violet Hunter

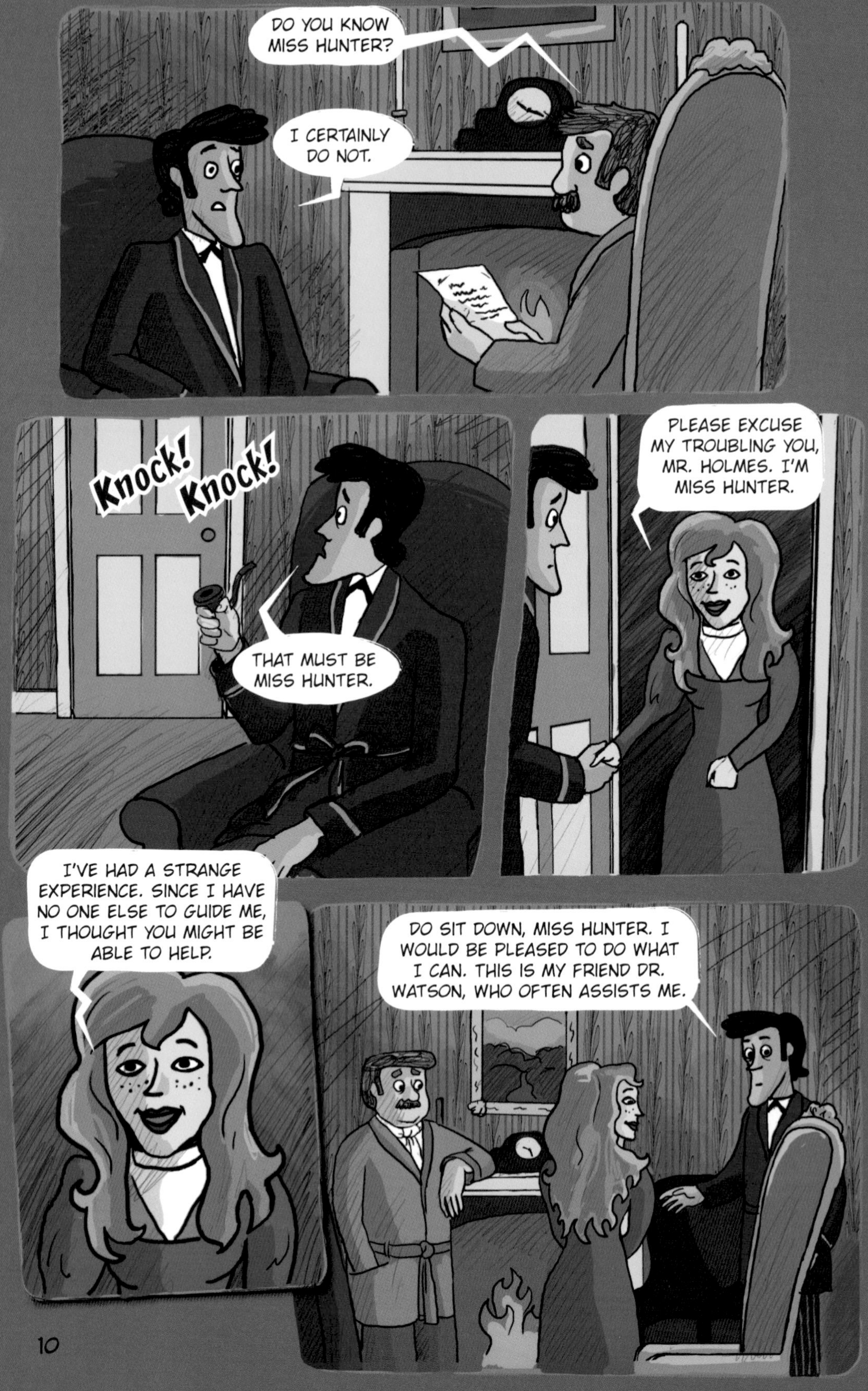
DO YOU KNOW MISS HUNTER?
I CERTAINLY DO NOT.
Knock! Knock!
THAT MUST BE MISS HUNTER.
PLEASE EXCUSE MY TROUBLING YOU, MR. HOLMES. I'M MISS HUNTER.
I'VE HAD A STRANGE EXPERIENCE. SINCE I HAVE NO ONE ELSE TO GUIDE ME, I THOUGHT YOU MIGHT BE ABLE TO HELP.
DO SIT DOWN, MISS HUNTER. I WOULD BE PLEASED TO DO WHAT I CAN. THIS IS MY FRIEND DR. WATSON, WHO OFTEN ASSISTS ME.

I could see that Holmes was impressed with Miss Hunter's manner and appearance. Sitting down in his chair, he asked for her to explain her situation. I settled back into my chair, wondering what she could possibly say that would intrigue him.

FOR THE PAST FIVE YEARS, I WAS A GOVERNESS FOR COLONEL SPENCE MUNRO. RECENTLY, HOWEVER, HE AND HIS FAMILY MOVED TO NOVA SCOTIA IN CANADA. I WAS FORCED TO SEEK NEW EMPLOYMENT.

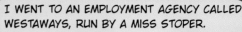
I WENT TO AN EMPLOYMENT AGENCY CALLED WESTAWAYS, RUN BY A MISS STOPER.

WESTAWAYS EMPLOYMENT AGENCY

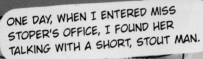
ONE DAY, WHEN I ENTERED MISS STOPER'S OFFICE, I FOUND HER TALKING WITH A SHORT, STOUT MAN.

WHEN HE SAW ME, HE SPRANG TO HIS FEET.

INDEED, THIS IS SHE! I COULD NOT ASK FOR ANYONE BETTER!

MISS, WOULD YOU CONSIDER A POSITION TAKING CARE OF EDWARD, MY SIX-YEAR-OLD SON?

I WAS RELIEVED TO BE ASKED ABOUT A POSITION, SO I SAID THAT I WOULD CONSIDER IT.

I MADE FOUR POUNDS A MONTH AT MY LAST POSITION.

MY, THAT'S A MERE PITTANCE FOR SOMEONE OF YOUR QUALITIES. YOU WILL BE RESPONSIBLE FOR THE EDUCATION OF A CHILD. THAT SURELY IS WORTH AT LEAST A HUNDRED POUNDS A YEAR.

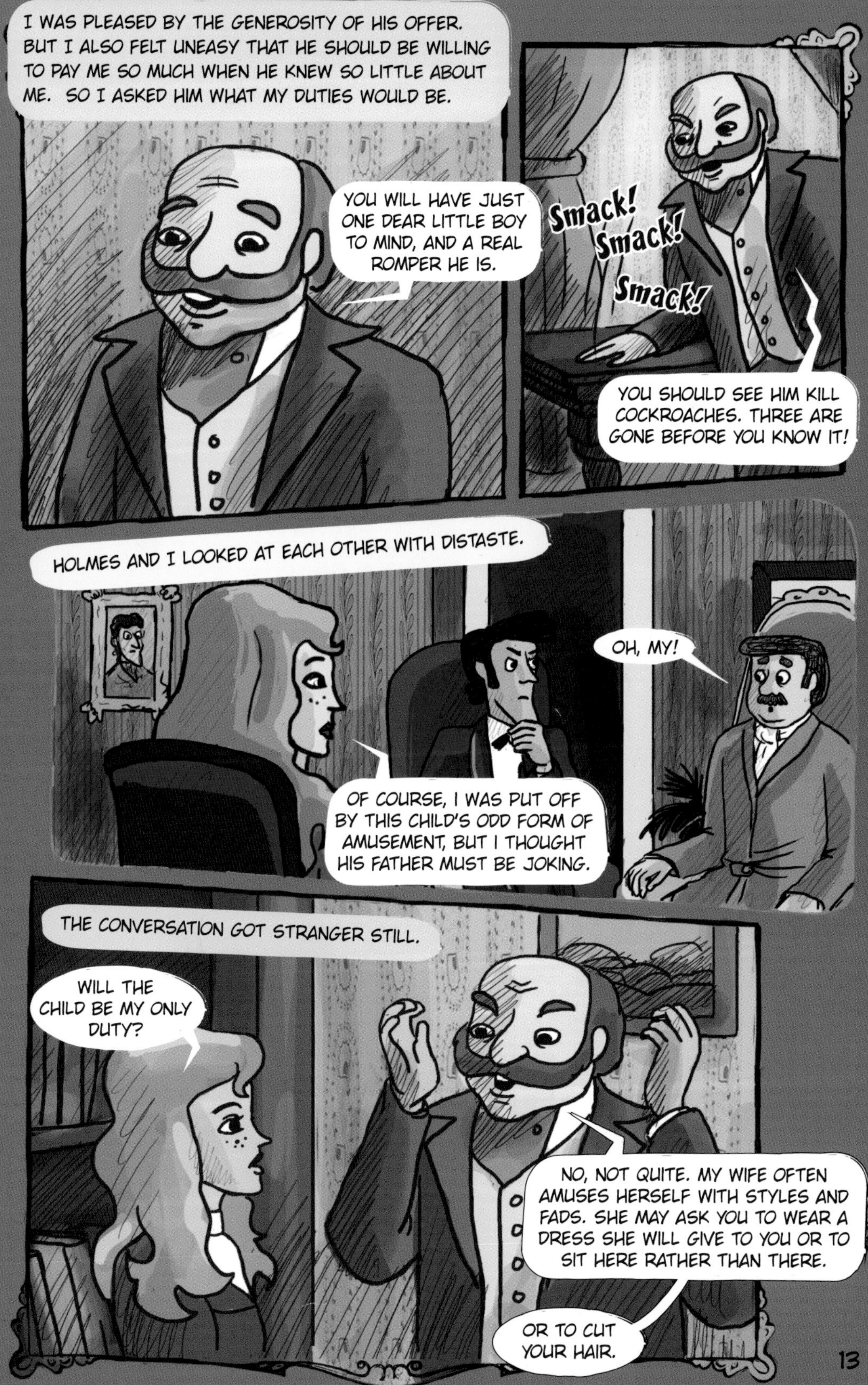
I WAS PLEASED BY THE GENEROSITY OF HIS OFFER. BUT I ALSO FELT UNEASY THAT HE SHOULD BE WILLING TO PAY ME SO MUCH WHEN HE KNEW SO LITTLE ABOUT ME. SO I ASKED HIM WHAT MY DUTIES WOULD BE.
YOU WILL HAVE JUST ONE DEAR LITTLE BOY TO MIND, AND A REAL ROMPER HE IS.
Smack!
Smack!
Smack!
YOU SHOULD SEE HIM KILL COCKROACHES. THREE ARE GONE BEFORE YOU KNOW IT!
HOLMES AND I LOOKED AT EACH OTHER WITH DISTASTE.
OH, MY!
OF COURSE, I WAS PUT OFF BY THIS CHILD'S ODD FORM OF AMUSEMENT, BUT I THOUGHT HIS FATHER MUST BE JOKING.
THE CONVERSATION GOT STRANGER STILL.
WILL THE CHILD BE MY ONLY DUTY?
NO, NOT QUITE. MY WIFE OFTEN AMUSES HERSELF WITH STYLES AND FADS. SHE MAY ASK YOU TO WEAR A DRESS SHE WILL GIVE TO YOU OR TO SIT HERE RATHER THAN THERE.
OR TO CUT YOUR HAIR.

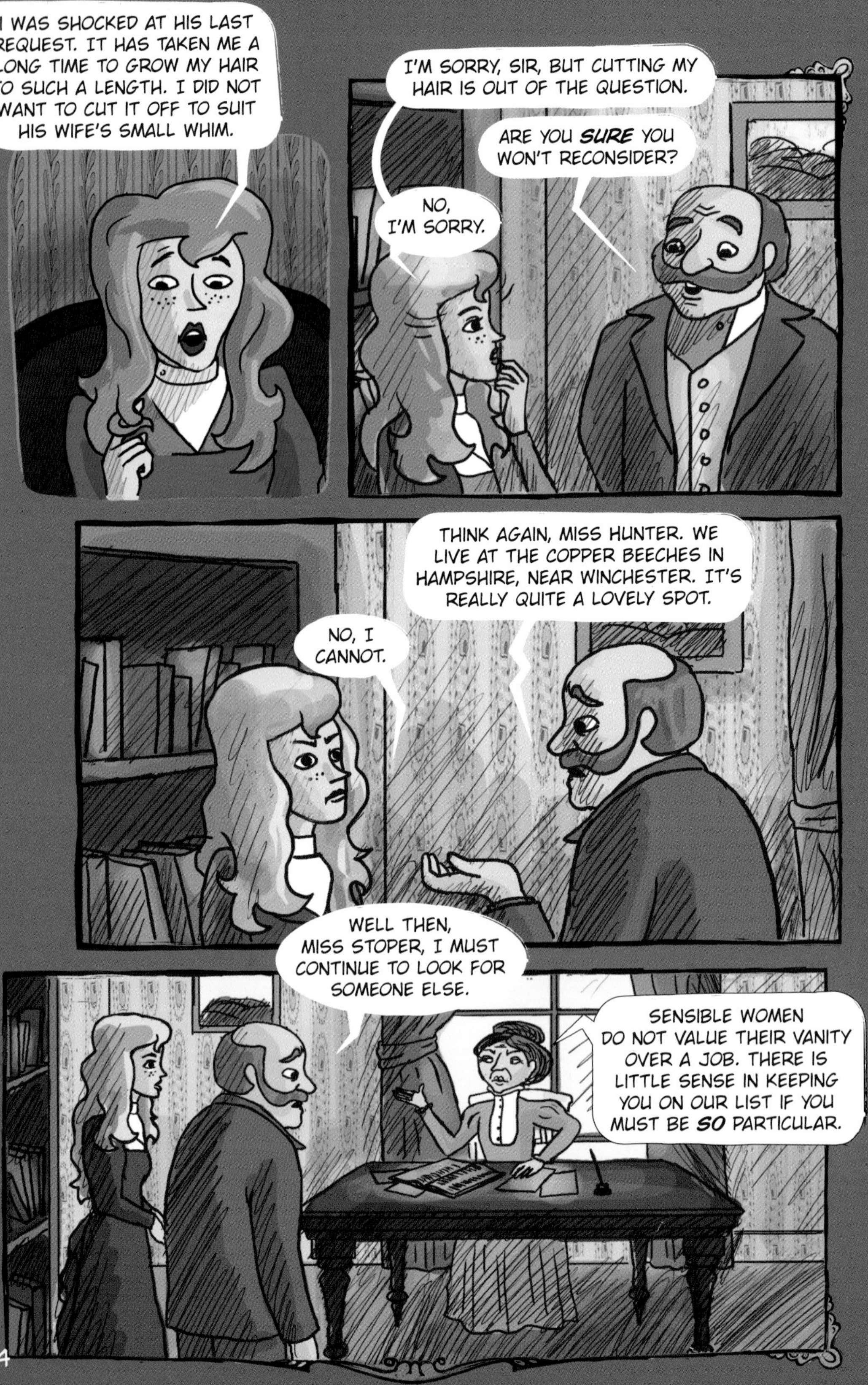
I WAS SHOCKED AT HIS LAST REQUEST. IT HAS TAKEN ME A LONG TIME TO GROW MY HAIR TO SUCH A LENGTH. I DID NOT WANT TO CUT IT OFF TO SUIT HIS WIFE'S SMALL WHIM.
I'M SORRY, SIR, BUT CUTTING MY HAIR IS OUT OF THE QUESTION.
ARE YOU *SURE* YOU WON'T RECONSIDER?
NO, I'M SORRY.
THINK AGAIN, MISS HUNTER. WE LIVE AT THE COPPER BEECHES IN HAMPSHIRE, NEAR WINCHESTER. IT'S REALLY QUITE A LOVELY SPOT.
NO, I CANNOT.
WELL THEN, MISS STOPER, I MUST CONTINUE TO LOOK FOR SOMEONE ELSE.
SENSIBLE WOMEN DO NOT VALUE THEIR VANITY OVER A JOB. THERE IS LITTLE SENSE IN KEEPING YOU ON OUR LIST IF YOU MUST BE *SO* PARTICULAR.

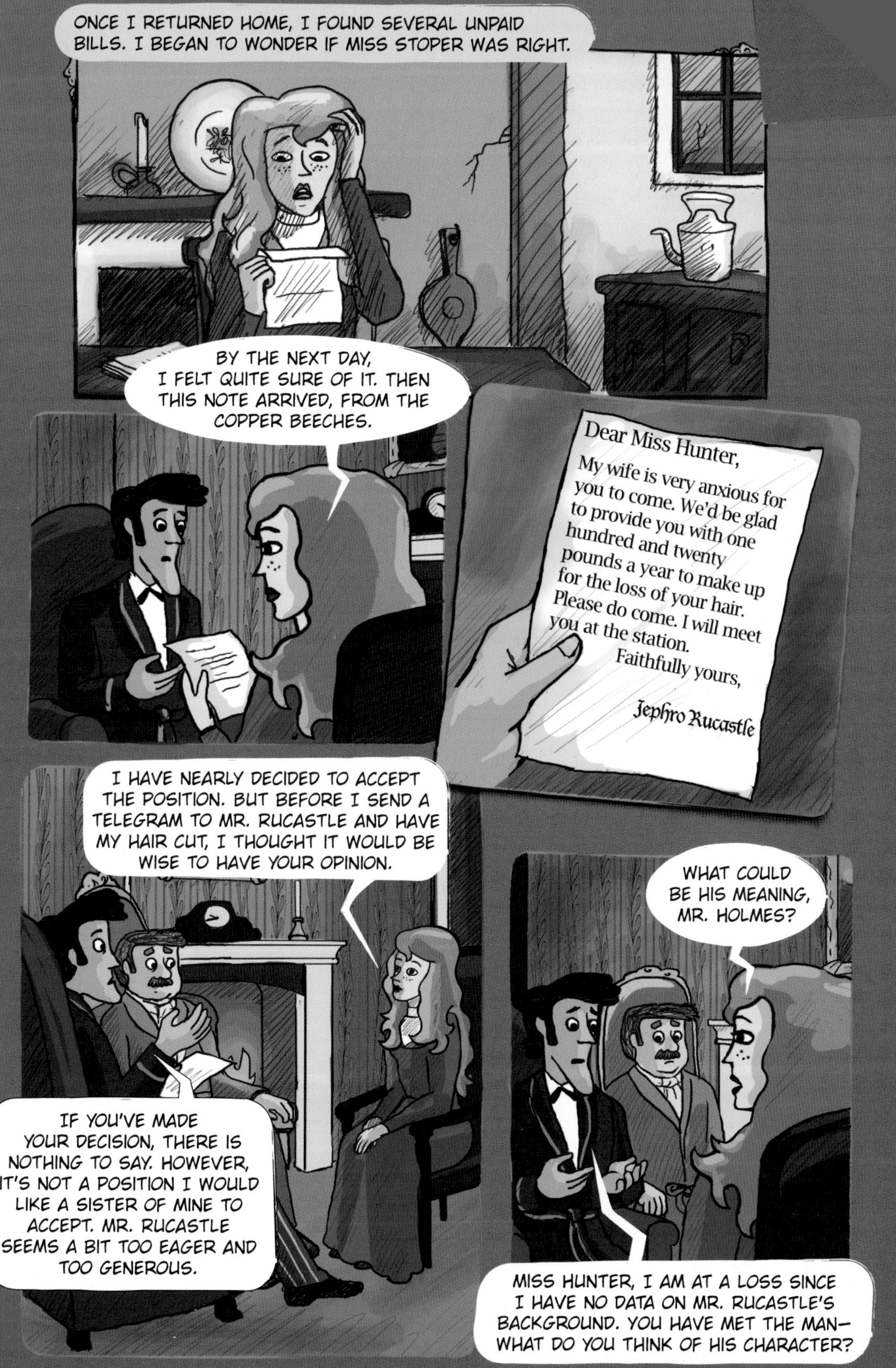

ONCE I RETURNED HOME, I FOUND SEVERAL UNPAID BILLS. I BEGAN TO WONDER IF MISS STOPER WAS RIGHT.
BY THE NEXT DAY, I FELT QUITE SURE OF IT. THEN THIS NOTE ARRIVED, FROM THE COPPER BEECHES.
Dear Miss Hunter,
My wife is very anxious for you to come. We'd be glad to provide you with one hundred and twenty pounds a year to make up for the loss of your hair. Please do come. I will meet you at the station.
Faithfully yours,
Jephro Rucastle
I HAVE NEARLY DECIDED TO ACCEPT THE POSITION. BUT BEFORE I SEND A TELEGRAM TO MR. RUCASTLE AND HAVE MY HAIR CUT, I THOUGHT IT WOULD BE WISE TO HAVE YOUR OPINION.
IF YOU'VE MADE YOUR DECISION, THERE IS NOTHING TO SAY. HOWEVER, IT'S NOT A POSITION I WOULD LIKE A SISTER OF MINE TO ACCEPT. MR. RUCASTLE SEEMS A BIT TOO EAGER AND TOO GENEROUS.
WHAT COULD BE HIS MEANING, MR. HOLMES?
MISS HUNTER, I AM AT A LOSS SINCE I HAVE NO DATA ON MR. RUCASTLE'S BACKGROUND. YOU HAVE MET THE MAN—WHAT DO YOU THINK OF HIS CHARACTER?

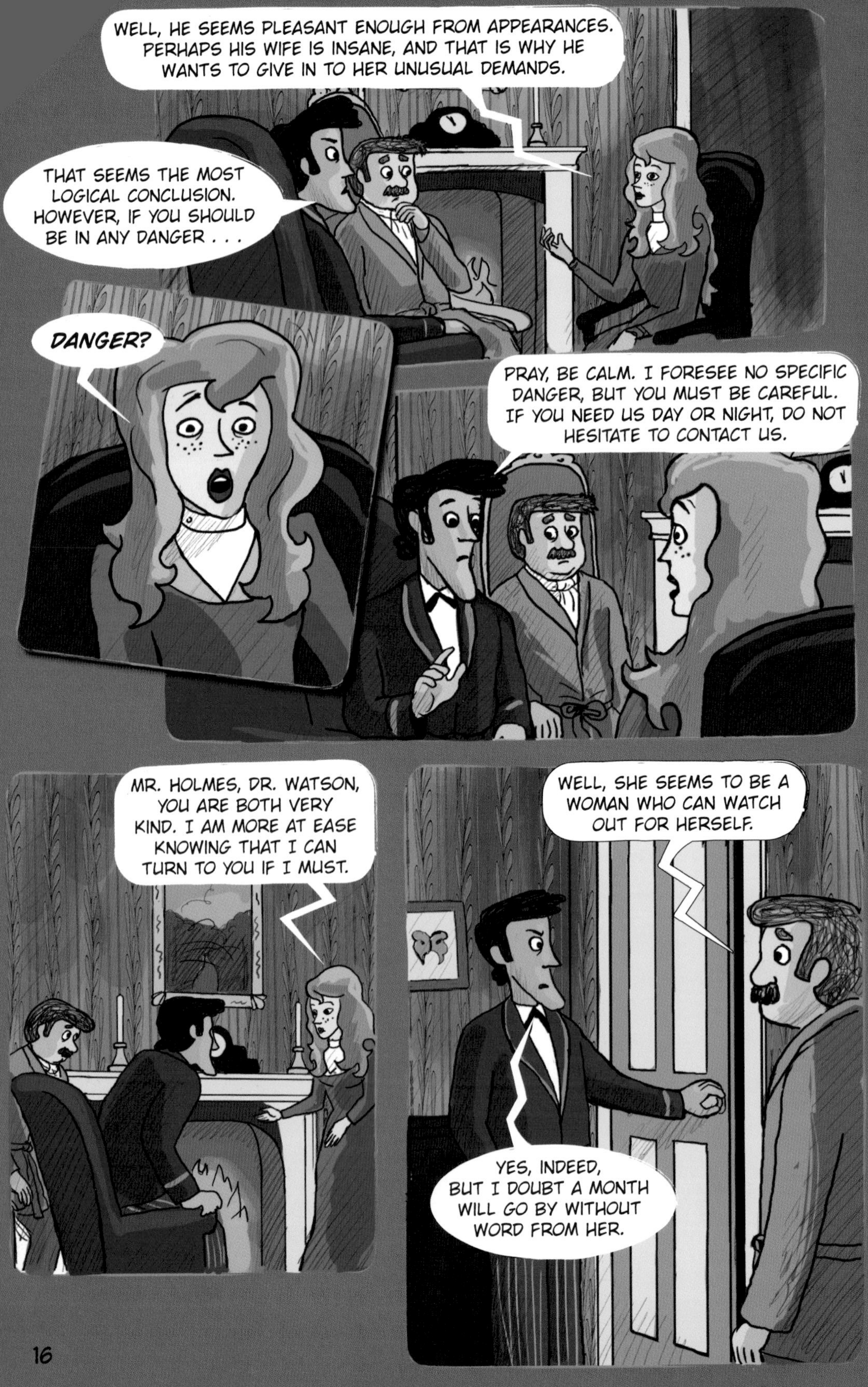
WELL, HE SEEMS PLEASANT ENOUGH FROM APPEARANCES. PERHAPS HIS WIFE IS INSANE, AND THAT IS WHY HE WANTS TO GIVE IN TO HER UNUSUAL DEMANDS.
THAT SEEMS THE MOST LOGICAL CONCLUSION. HOWEVER, IF YOU SHOULD BE IN ANY DANGER . . .
DANGER?
PRAY, BE CALM. I FORESEE NO SPECIFIC DANGER, BUT YOU MUST BE CAREFUL. IF YOU NEED US DAY OR NIGHT, DO NOT HESITATE TO CONTACT US.
MR. HOLMES, DR. WATSON, YOU ARE BOTH VERY KIND. I AM MORE AT EASE KNOWING THAT I CAN TURN TO YOU IF I MUST.
WELL, SHE SEEMS TO BE A WOMAN WHO CAN WATCH OUT FOR HERSELF.
YES, INDEED, BUT I DOUBT A MONTH WILL GO BY WITHOUT WORD FROM HER.

April 27, 1894, 9:30 a.m.

Three weeks later, a telegram from Miss Hunter arrived, just as Holmes had predicted. We had both risen early and were sitting down to breakfast. Holmes read the brief message aloud. Miss Hunter wished that we meet her at the Black Swan Hotel that day. I pulled out my pocket watch to check the time.

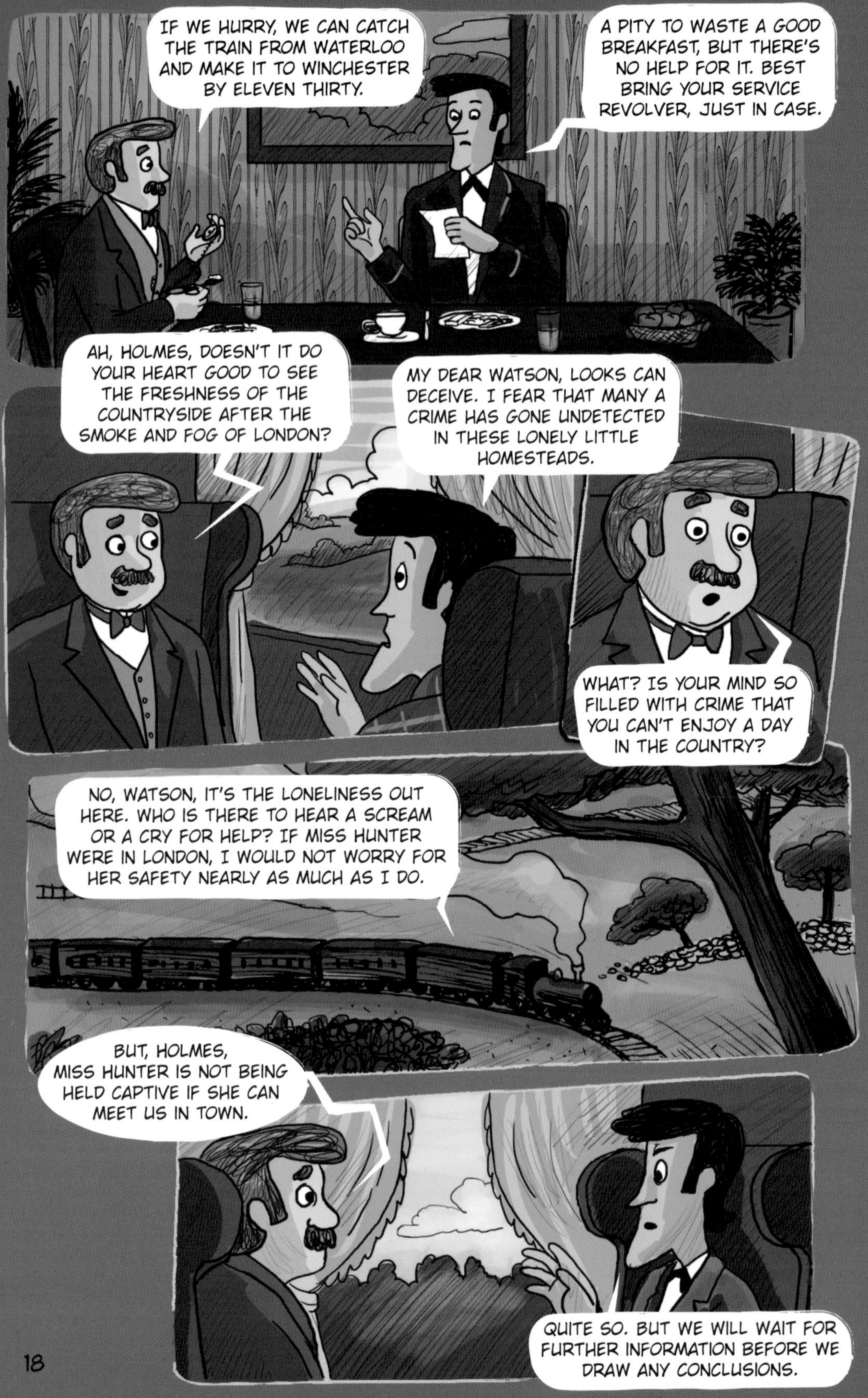
IF WE HURRY, WE CAN CATCH THE TRAIN FROM WATERLOO AND MAKE IT TO WINCHESTER BY ELEVEN THIRTY.
A PITY TO WASTE A GOOD BREAKFAST, BUT THERE'S NO HELP FOR IT. BEST BRING YOUR SERVICE REVOLVER, JUST IN CASE.
AH, HOLMES, DOESN'T IT DO YOUR HEART GOOD TO SEE THE FRESHNESS OF THE COUNTRYSIDE AFTER THE SMOKE AND FOG OF LONDON?
MY DEAR WATSON, LOOKS CAN DECEIVE. I FEAR THAT MANY A CRIME HAS GONE UNDETECTED IN THESE LONELY LITTLE HOMESTEADS.
WHAT? IS YOUR MIND SO FILLED WITH CRIME THAT YOU CAN'T ENJOY A DAY IN THE COUNTRY?
NO, WATSON, IT'S THE LONELINESS OUT HERE. WHO IS THERE TO HEAR A SCREAM OR A CRY FOR HELP? IF MISS HUNTER WERE IN LONDON, I WOULD NOT WORRY FOR HER SAFETY NEARLY AS MUCH AS I DO.
BUT, HOLMES, MISS HUNTER IS NOT BEING HELD CAPTIVE IF SHE CAN MEET US IN TOWN.
QUITE SO. BUT WE WILL WAIT FOR FURTHER INFORMATION BEFORE WE DRAW ANY CONCLUSIONS.

April 27, 1894, 11:30 a.m.

Winchester Cathedral soon came into view. Within a quarter of an hour, we had found our way to the Black Swan Hotel in the middle of the High Street. Miss Hunter was waiting inside a sitting room.

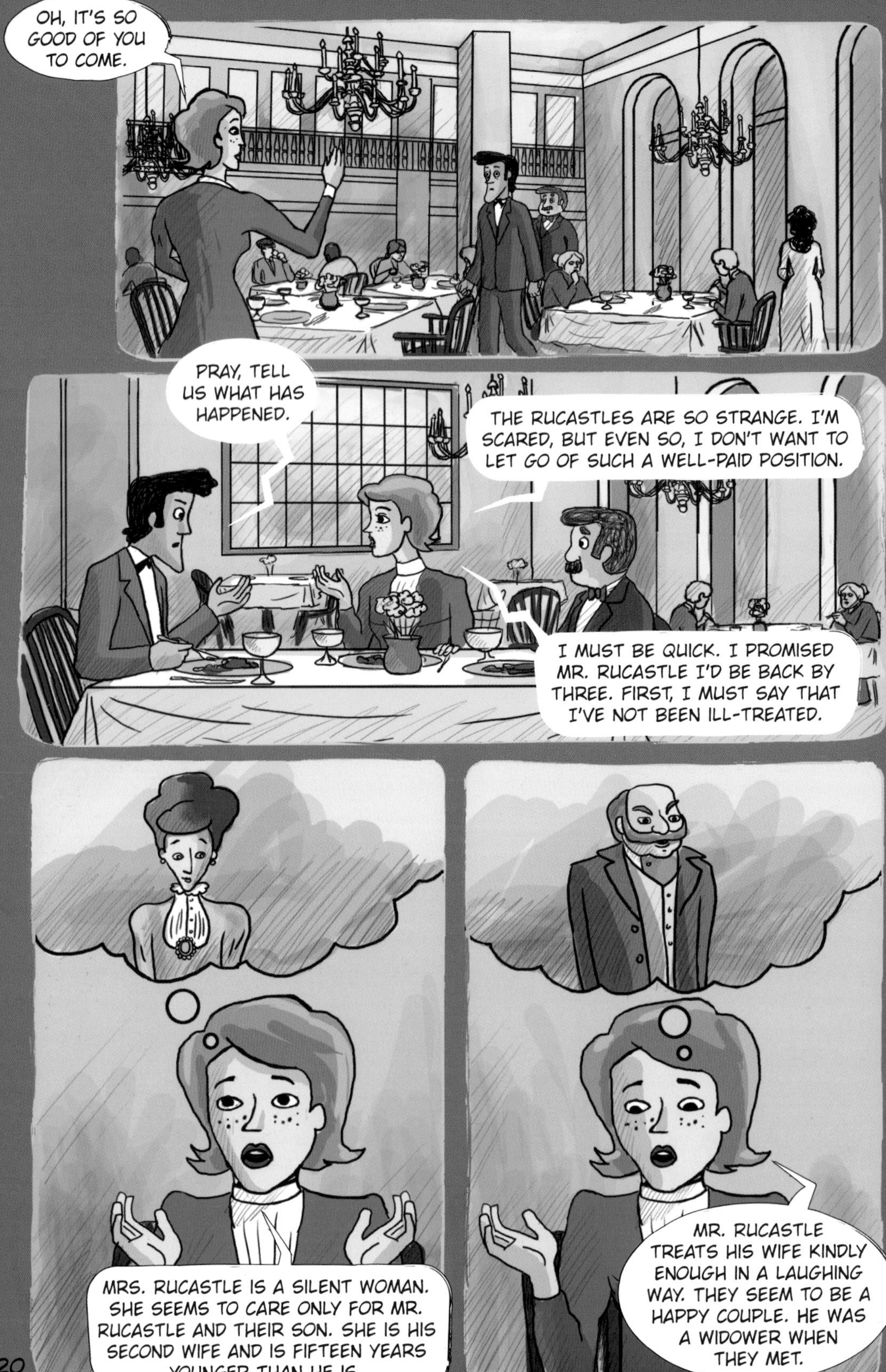
OH, IT'S SO GOOD OF YOU TO COME.
PRAY, TELL US WHAT HAS HAPPENED.
THE RUCASTLES ARE SO STRANGE. I'M SCARED, BUT EVEN SO, I DON'T WANT TO LET GO OF SUCH A WELL-PAID POSITION.
I MUST BE QUICK. I PROMISED MR. RUCASTLE I'D BE BACK BY THREE. FIRST, I MUST SAY THAT I'VE NOT BEEN ILL-TREATED.
MRS. RUCASTLE IS A SILENT WOMAN. SHE SEEMS TO CARE ONLY FOR MR. RUCASTLE AND THEIR SON. SHE IS HIS SECOND WIFE AND IS FIFTEEN YEARS YOUNGER THAN HE IS.
MR. RUCASTLE TREATS HIS WIFE KINDLY ENOUGH IN A LAUGHING WAY. THEY SEEM TO BE A HAPPY COUPLE. HE WAS A WIDOWER WHEN THEY MET.

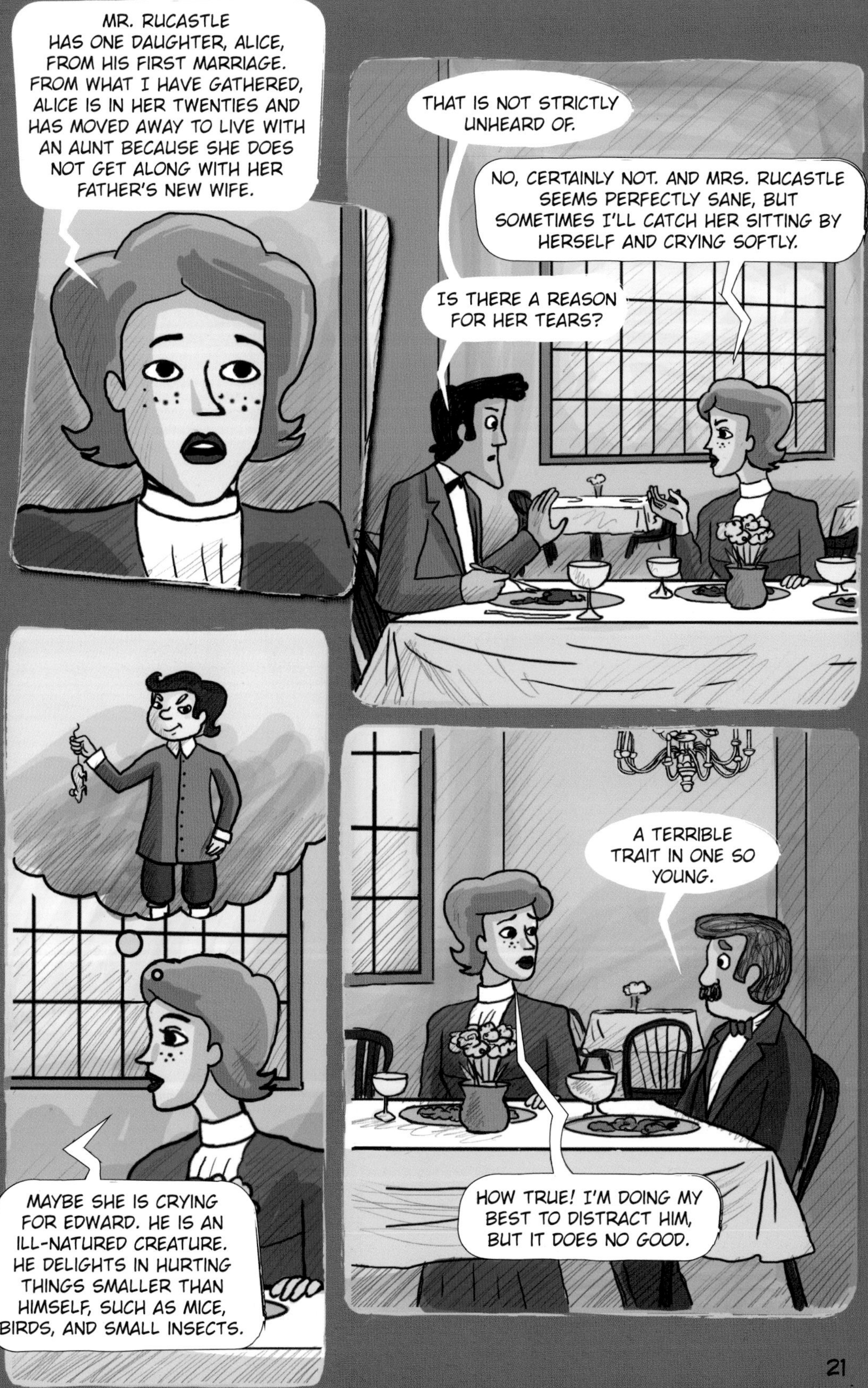
MR. RUCASTLE HAS ONE DAUGHTER, ALICE, FROM HIS FIRST MARRIAGE. FROM WHAT I HAVE GATHERED, ALICE IS IN HER TWENTIES AND HAS MOVED AWAY TO LIVE WITH AN AUNT BECAUSE SHE DOES NOT GET ALONG WITH HER FATHER'S NEW WIFE.
THAT IS NOT STRICTLY UNHEARD OF.
NO, CERTAINLY NOT. AND MRS. RUCASTLE SEEMS PERFECTLY SANE, BUT SOMETIMES I'LL CATCH HER SITTING BY HERSELF AND CRYING SOFTLY.
IS THERE A REASON FOR HER TEARS?
MAYBE SHE IS CRYING FOR EDWARD. HE IS AN ILL-NATURED CREATURE. HE DELIGHTS IN HURTING THINGS SMALLER THAN HIMSELF, SUCH AS MICE, BIRDS, AND SMALL INSECTS.
A TERRIBLE TRAIT IN ONE SO YOUNG.
HOW TRUE! I'M DOING MY BEST TO DISTRACT HIM, BUT IT DOES NO GOOD.

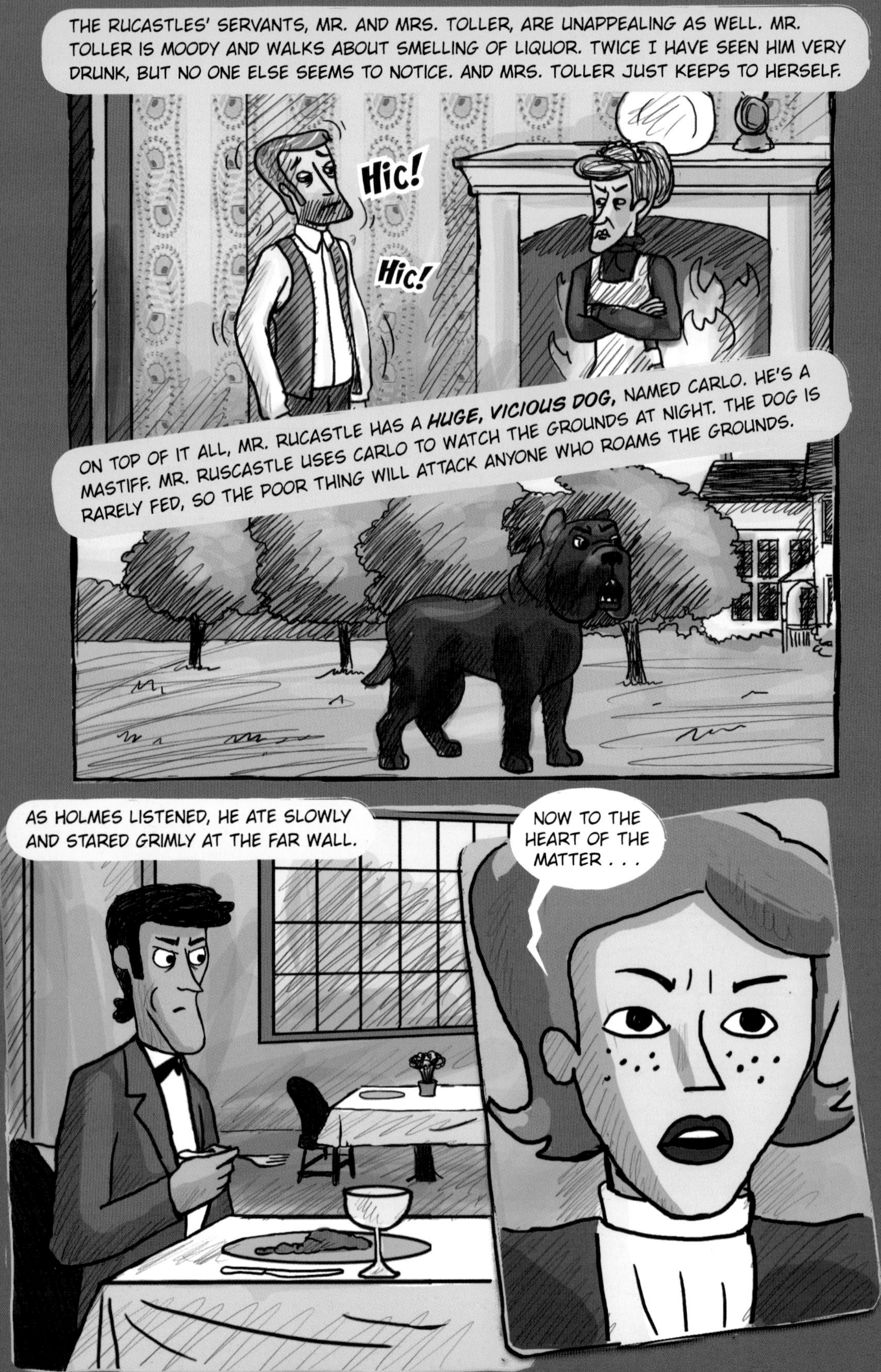
THE RUCASTLES' SERVANTS, MR. AND MRS. TOLLER, ARE UNAPPEALING AS WELL. MR. TOLLER IS MOODY AND WALKS ABOUT SMELLING OF LIQUOR. TWICE I HAVE SEEN HIM VERY DRUNK, BUT NO ONE ELSE SEEMS TO NOTICE. AND MRS. TOLLER JUST KEEPS TO HERSELF.
Hic!
Hic!
ON TOP OF IT ALL, MR. RUCASTLE HAS A **HUGE, VICIOUS DOG,** NAMED CARLO. HE'S A MASTIFF. MR. RUSCASTLE USES CARLO TO WATCH THE GROUNDS AT NIGHT. THE DOG IS RARELY FED, SO THE POOR THING WILL ATTACK ANYONE WHO ROAMS THE GROUNDS.
AS HOLMES LISTENED, HE ATE SLOWLY AND STARED GRIMLY AT THE FAR WALL.
NOW TO THE HEART OF THE MATTER . . .

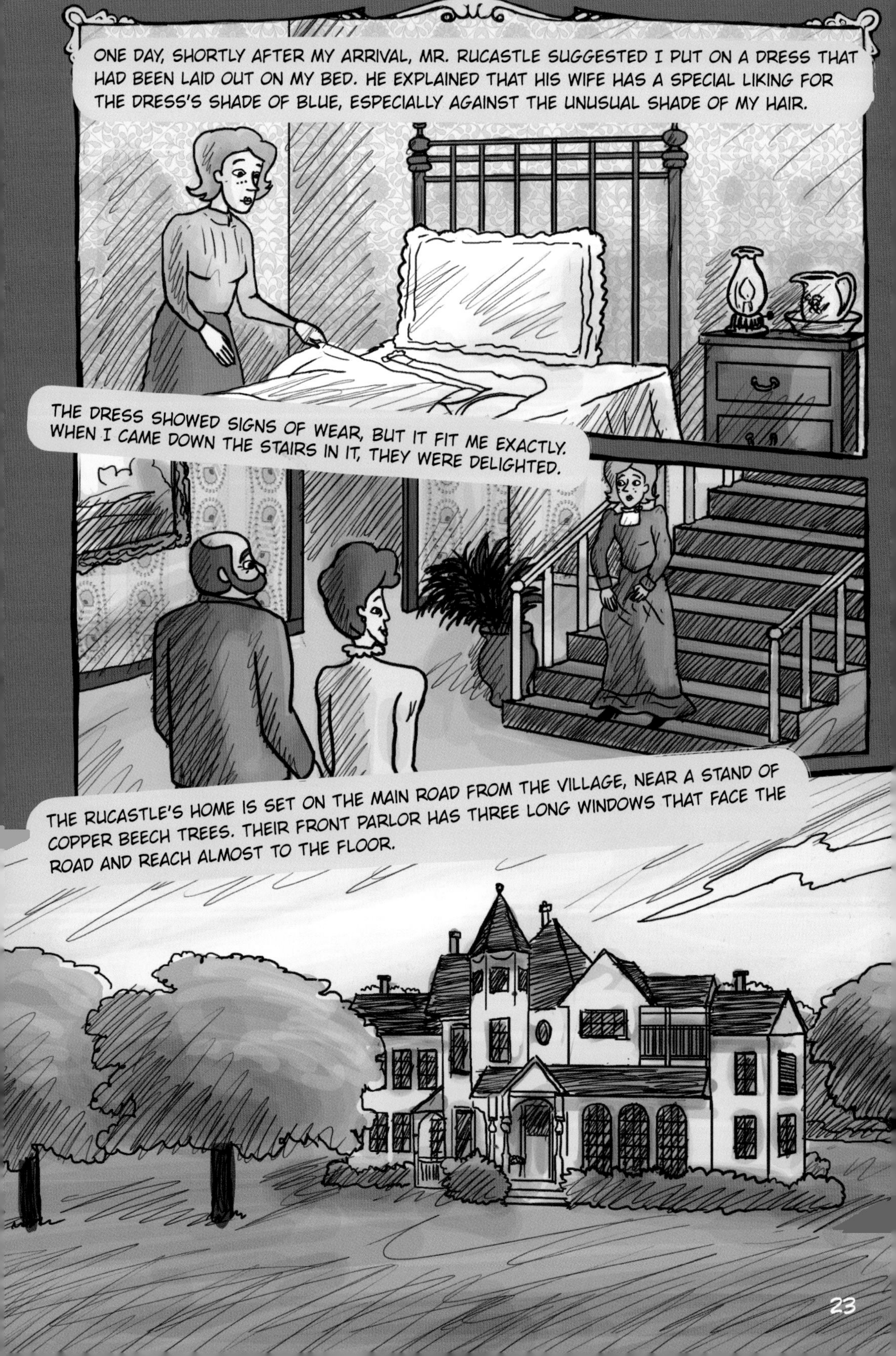
ONE DAY, SHORTLY AFTER MY ARRIVAL, MR. RUCASTLE SUGGESTED I PUT ON A DRESS THAT HAD BEEN LAID OUT ON MY BED. HE EXPLAINED THAT HIS WIFE HAS A SPECIAL LIKING FOR THE DRESS'S SHADE OF BLUE, ESPECIALLY AGAINST THE UNUSUAL SHADE OF MY HAIR.
THE DRESS SHOWED SIGNS OF WEAR, BUT IT FIT ME EXACTLY. WHEN I CAME DOWN THE STAIRS IN IT, THEY WERE DELIGHTED.
THE RUCASTLE'S HOME IS SET ON THE MAIN ROAD FROM THE VILLAGE, NEAR A STAND OF COPPER BEECH TREES. THEIR FRONT PARLOR HAS THREE LONG WINDOWS THAT FACE THE ROAD AND REACH ALMOST TO THE FLOOR.

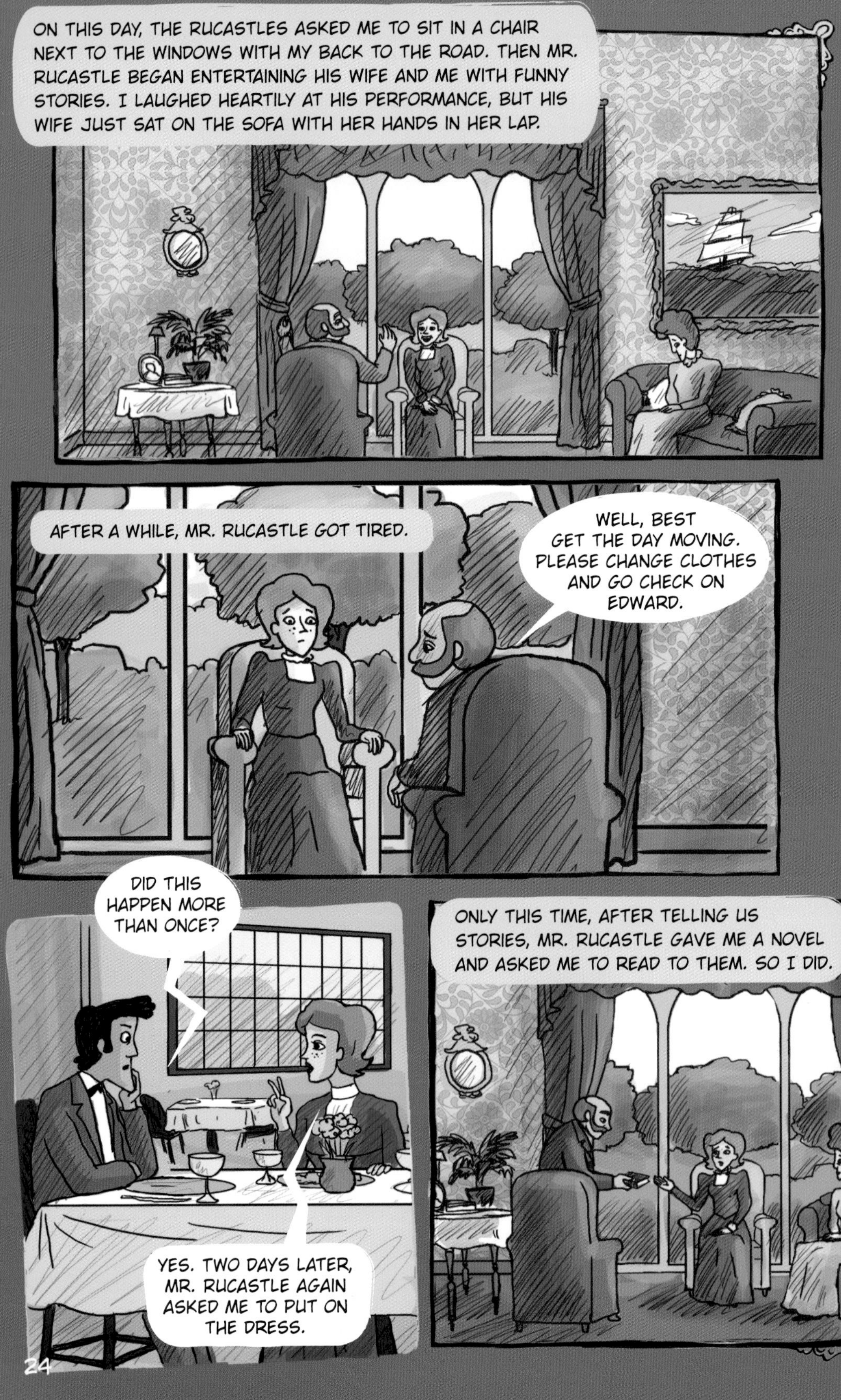

ON THIS DAY, THE RUCASTLES ASKED ME TO SIT IN A CHAIR NEXT TO THE WINDOWS WITH MY BACK TO THE ROAD. THEN MR. RUCASTLE BEGAN ENTERTAINING HIS WIFE AND ME WITH FUNNY STORIES. I LAUGHED HEARTILY AT HIS PERFORMANCE, BUT HIS WIFE JUST SAT ON THE SOFA WITH HER HANDS IN HER LAP.
AFTER A WHILE, MR. RUCASTLE GOT TIRED.
WELL, BEST GET THE DAY MOVING. PLEASE CHANGE CLOTHES AND GO CHECK ON EDWARD.
DID THIS HAPPEN MORE THAN ONCE?
YES. TWO DAYS LATER, MR. RUCASTLE AGAIN ASKED ME TO PUT ON THE DRESS.
ONLY THIS TIME, AFTER TELLING US STORIES, MR. RUCASTLE GAVE ME A NOVEL AND ASKED ME TO READ TO THEM. SO I DID.

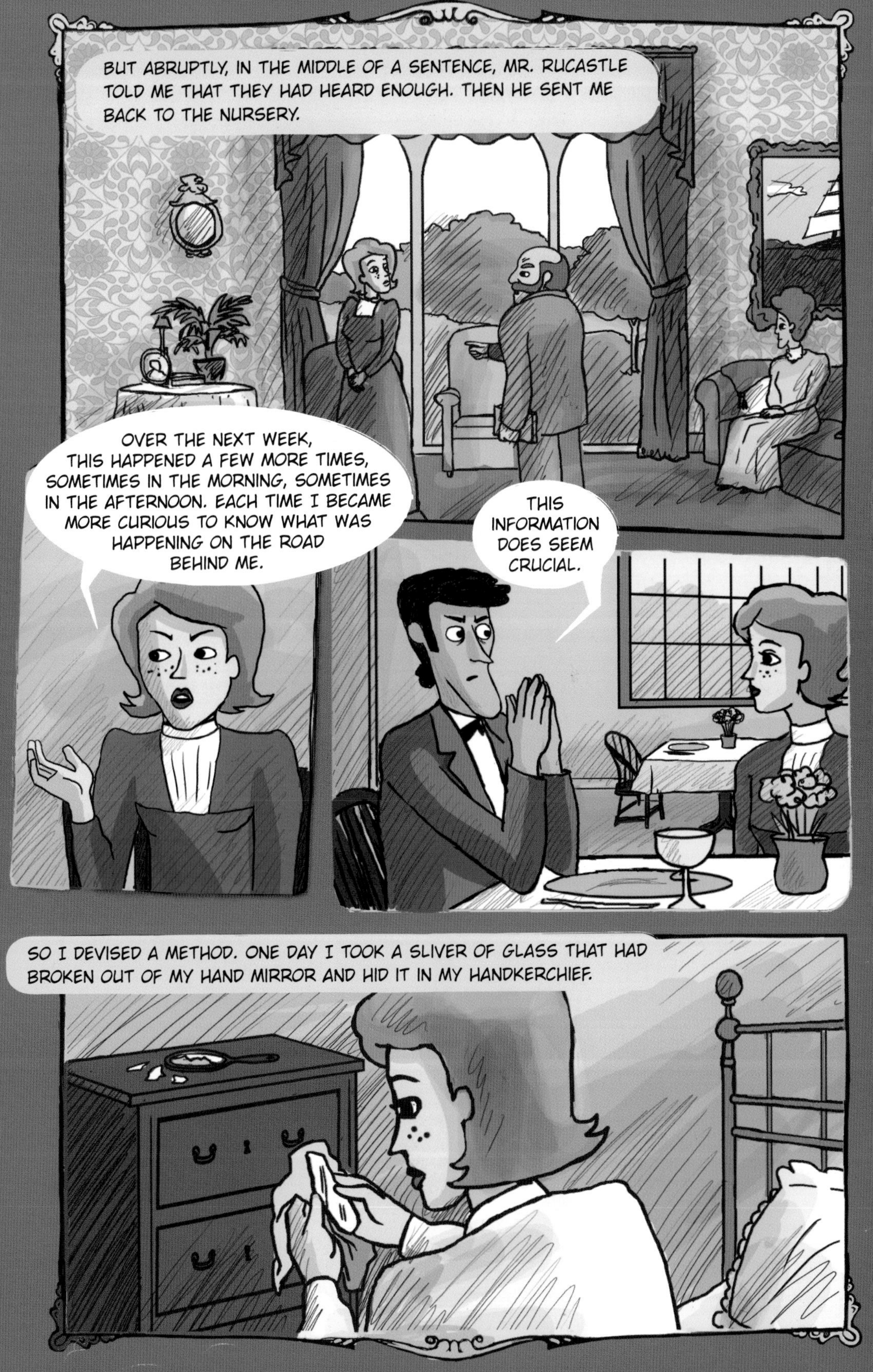
BUT ABRUPTLY, IN THE MIDDLE OF A SENTENCE, MR. RUCASTLE TOLD ME THAT THEY HAD HEARD ENOUGH. THEN HE SENT ME BACK TO THE NURSERY.
OVER THE NEXT WEEK, THIS HAPPENED A FEW MORE TIMES, SOMETIMES IN THE MORNING, SOMETIMES IN THE AFTERNOON. EACH TIME I BECAME MORE CURIOUS TO KNOW WHAT WAS HAPPENING ON THE ROAD BEHIND ME.
THIS INFORMATION DOES SEEM CRUCIAL.
SO I DEVISED A METHOD. ONE DAY I TOOK A SLIVER OF GLASS THAT HAD BROKEN OUT OF MY HAND MIRROR AND HID IT IN MY HANDKERCHIEF.

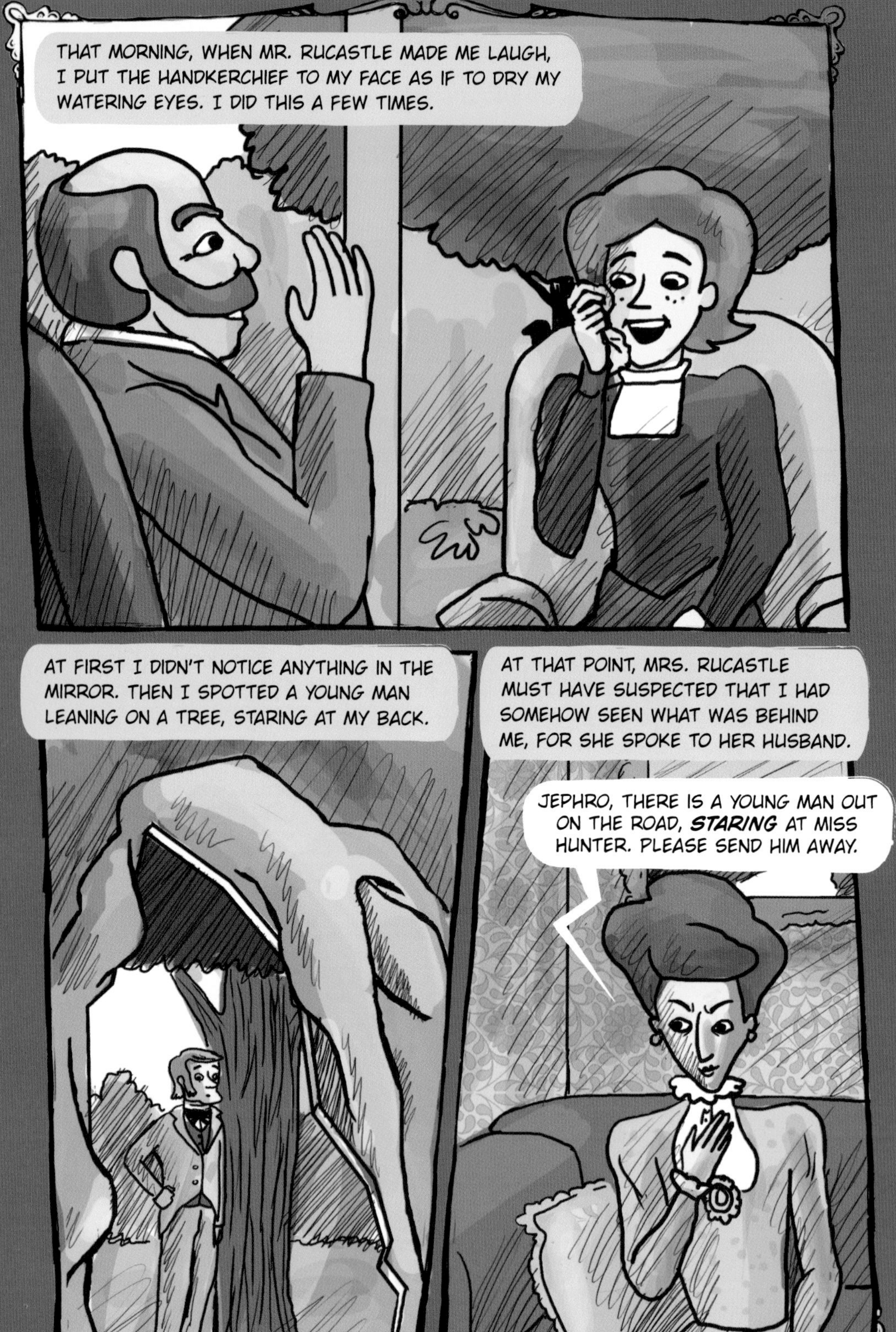
THAT MORNING, WHEN MR. RUCASTLE MADE ME LAUGH, I PUT THE HANDKERCHIEF TO MY FACE AS IF TO DRY MY WATERING EYES. I DID THIS A FEW TIMES.
AT FIRST I DIDN'T NOTICE ANYTHING IN THE MIRROR. THEN I SPOTTED A YOUNG MAN LEANING ON A TREE, STARING AT MY BACK.
AT THAT POINT, MRS. RUCASTLE MUST HAVE SUSPECTED THAT I HAD SOMEHOW SEEN WHAT WAS BEHIND ME, FOR SHE SPOKE TO HER HUSBAND.
JEPHRO, THERE IS A YOUNG MAN OUT ON THE ROAD, STARING AT MISS HUNTER. PLEASE SEND HIM AWAY.

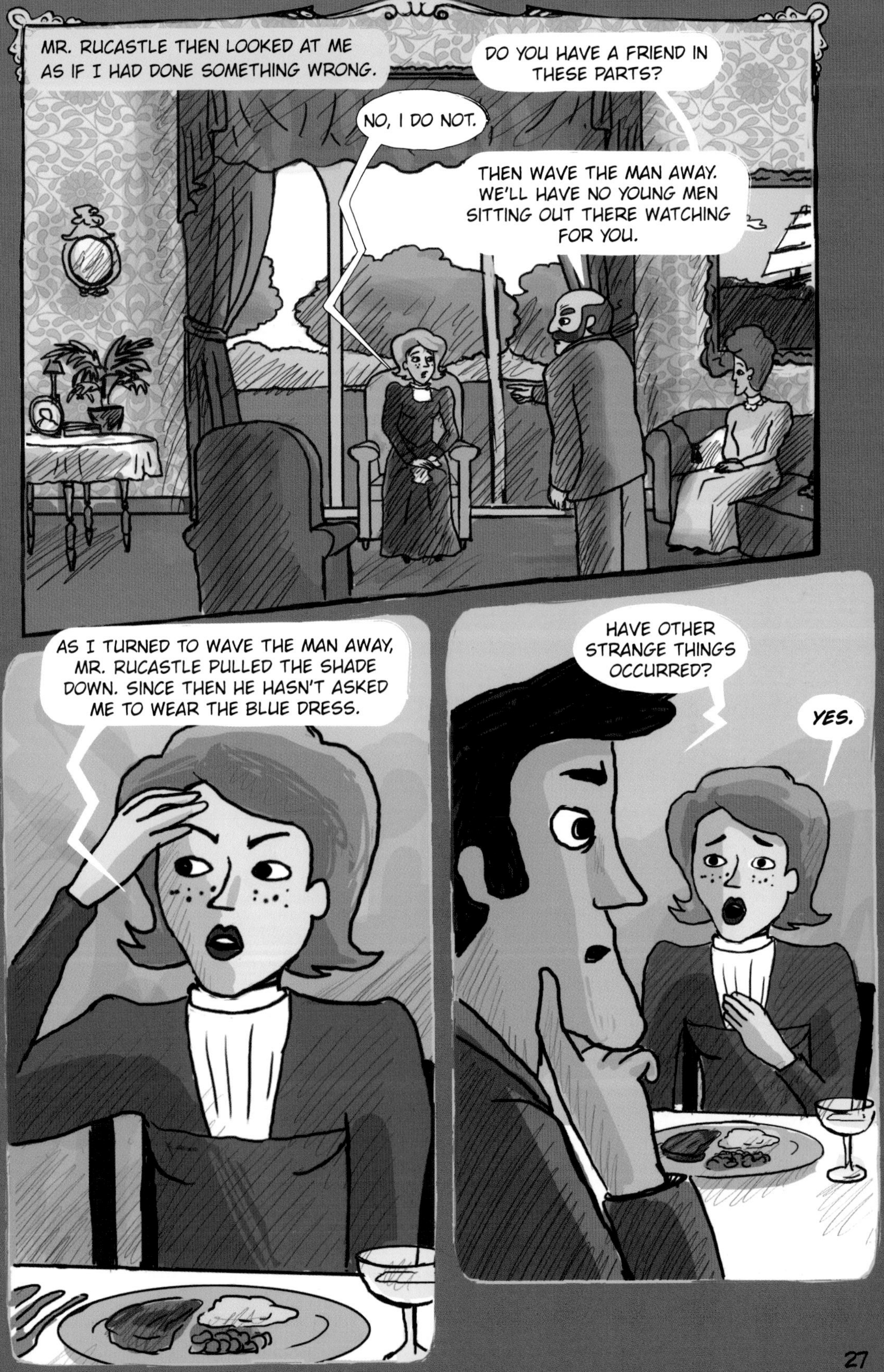
MR. RUCASTLE THEN LOOKED AT ME AS IF I HAD DONE SOMETHING WRONG.
DO YOU HAVE A FRIEND IN THESE PARTS?
NO, I DO NOT.
THEN WAVE THE MAN AWAY. WE'LL HAVE NO YOUNG MEN SITTING OUT THERE WATCHING FOR YOU.
AS I TURNED TO WAVE THE MAN AWAY, MR. RUCASTLE PULLED THE SHADE DOWN. SINCE THEN HE HASN'T ASKED ME TO WEAR THE BLUE DRESS.
HAVE OTHER STRANGE THINGS OCCURRED?
YES.

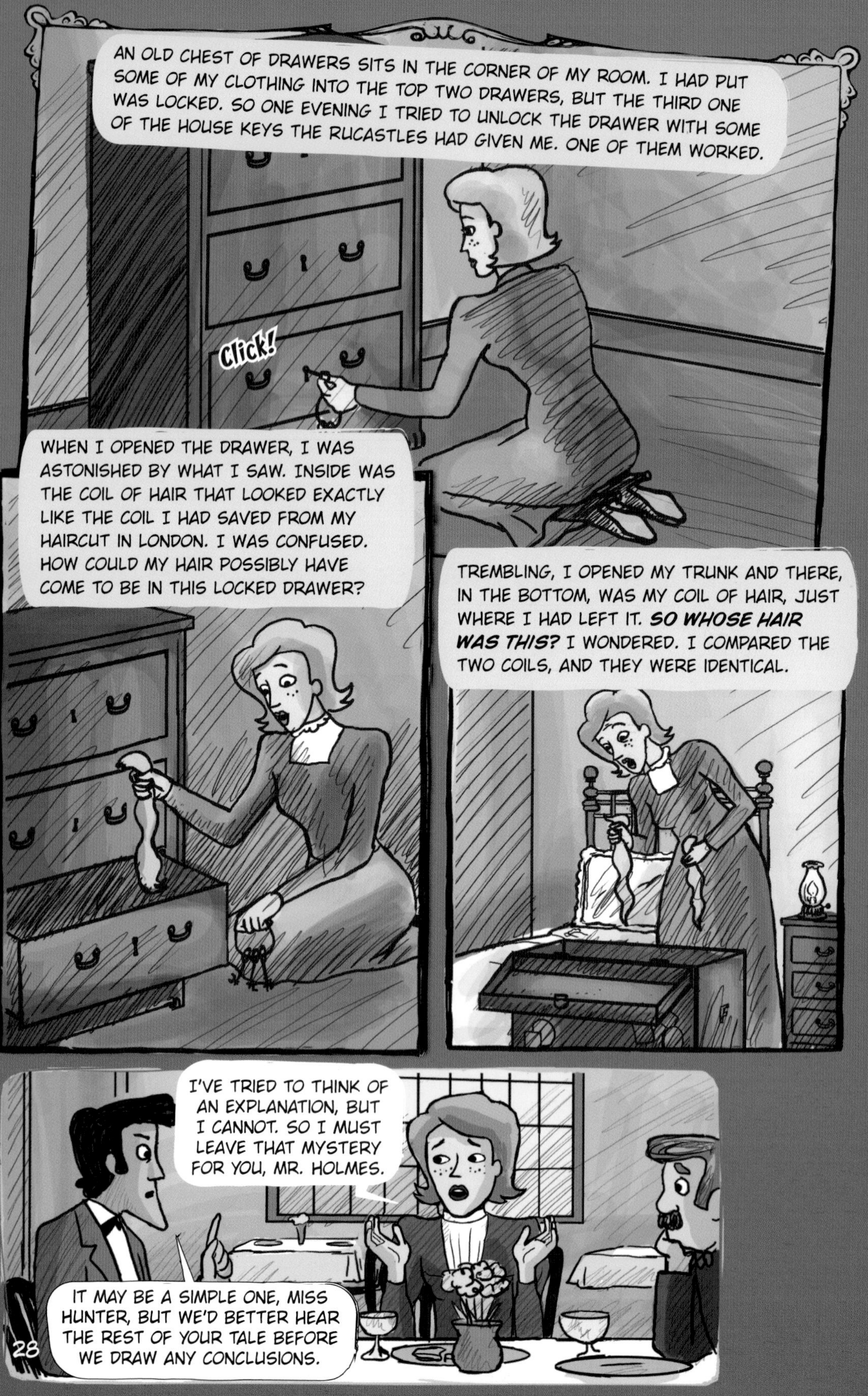
AN OLD CHEST OF DRAWERS SITS IN THE CORNER OF MY ROOM. I HAD PUT SOME OF MY CLOTHING INTO THE TOP TWO DRAWERS, BUT THE THIRD ONE WAS LOCKED. SO ONE EVENING I TRIED TO UNLOCK THE DRAWER WITH SOME OF THE HOUSE KEYS THE RUCASTLES HAD GIVEN ME. ONE OF THEM WORKED.
Click!
WHEN I OPENED THE DRAWER, I WAS ASTONISHED BY WHAT I SAW. INSIDE WAS THE COIL OF HAIR THAT LOOKED EXACTLY LIKE THE COIL I HAD SAVED FROM MY HAIRCUT IN LONDON. I WAS CONFUSED. HOW COULD MY HAIR POSSIBLY HAVE COME TO BE IN THIS LOCKED DRAWER?
TREMBLING, I OPENED MY TRUNK AND THERE, IN THE BOTTOM, WAS MY COIL OF HAIR, JUST WHERE I HAD LEFT IT. ***SO WHOSE HAIR WAS THIS?*** I WONDERED. I COMPARED THE TWO COILS, AND THEY WERE IDENTICAL.
I'VE TRIED TO THINK OF AN EXPLANATION, BUT I CANNOT. SO I MUST LEAVE THAT MYSTERY FOR YOU, MR. HOLMES.
IT MAY BE A SIMPLE ONE, MISS HUNTER, BUT WE'D BETTER HEAR THE REST OF YOUR TALE BEFORE WE DRAW ANY CONCLUSIONS.

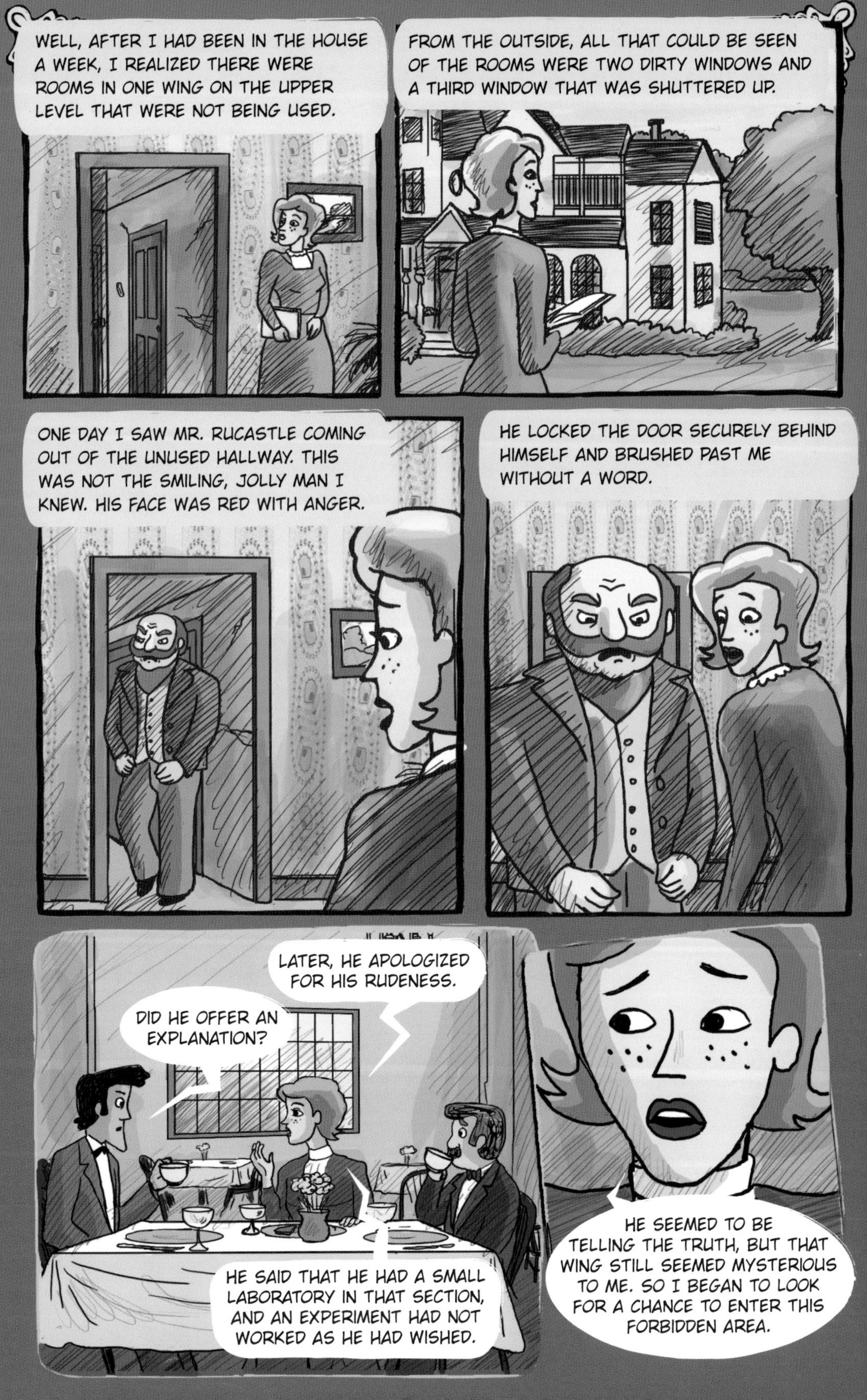
WELL, AFTER I HAD BEEN IN THE HOUSE A WEEK, I REALIZED THERE WERE ROOMS IN ONE WING ON THE UPPER LEVEL THAT WERE NOT BEING USED.
FROM THE OUTSIDE, ALL THAT COULD BE SEEN OF THE ROOMS WERE TWO DIRTY WINDOWS AND A THIRD WINDOW THAT WAS SHUTTERED UP.
ONE DAY I SAW MR. RUCASTLE COMING OUT OF THE UNUSED HALLWAY. THIS WAS NOT THE SMILING, JOLLY MAN I KNEW. HIS FACE WAS RED WITH ANGER.
HE LOCKED THE DOOR SECURELY BEHIND HIMSELF AND BRUSHED PAST ME WITHOUT A WORD.
LATER, HE APOLOGIZED FOR HIS RUDENESS.
DID HE OFFER AN EXPLANATION?
HE SAID THAT HE HAD A SMALL LABORATORY IN THAT SECTION, AND AN EXPERIMENT HAD NOT WORKED AS HE HAD WISHED.
HE SEEMED TO BE TELLING THE TRUTH, BUT THAT WING STILL SEEMED MYSTERIOUS TO ME. SO I BEGAN TO LOOK FOR A CHANCE TO ENTER THIS FORBIDDEN AREA.

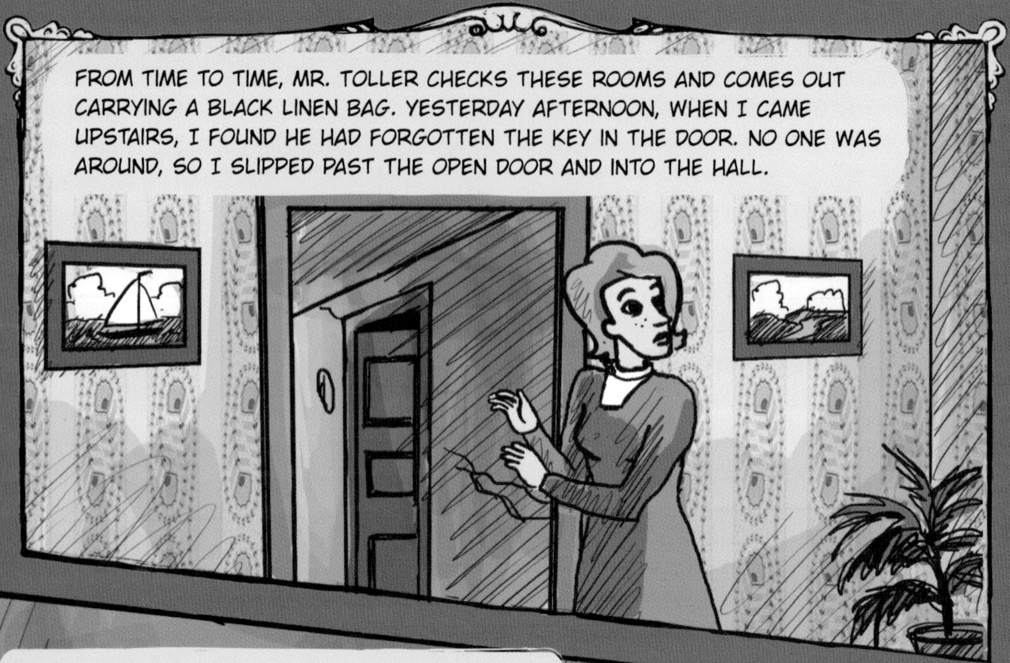
FROM TIME TO TIME, MR. TOLLER CHECKS THESE ROOMS AND COMES OUT CARRYING A BLACK LINEN BAG. YESTERDAY AFTERNOON, WHEN I CAME UPSTAIRS, I FOUND HE HAD FORGOTTEN THE KEY IN THE DOOR. NO ONE WAS AROUND, SO I SLIPPED PAST THE OPEN DOOR AND INTO THE HALL.

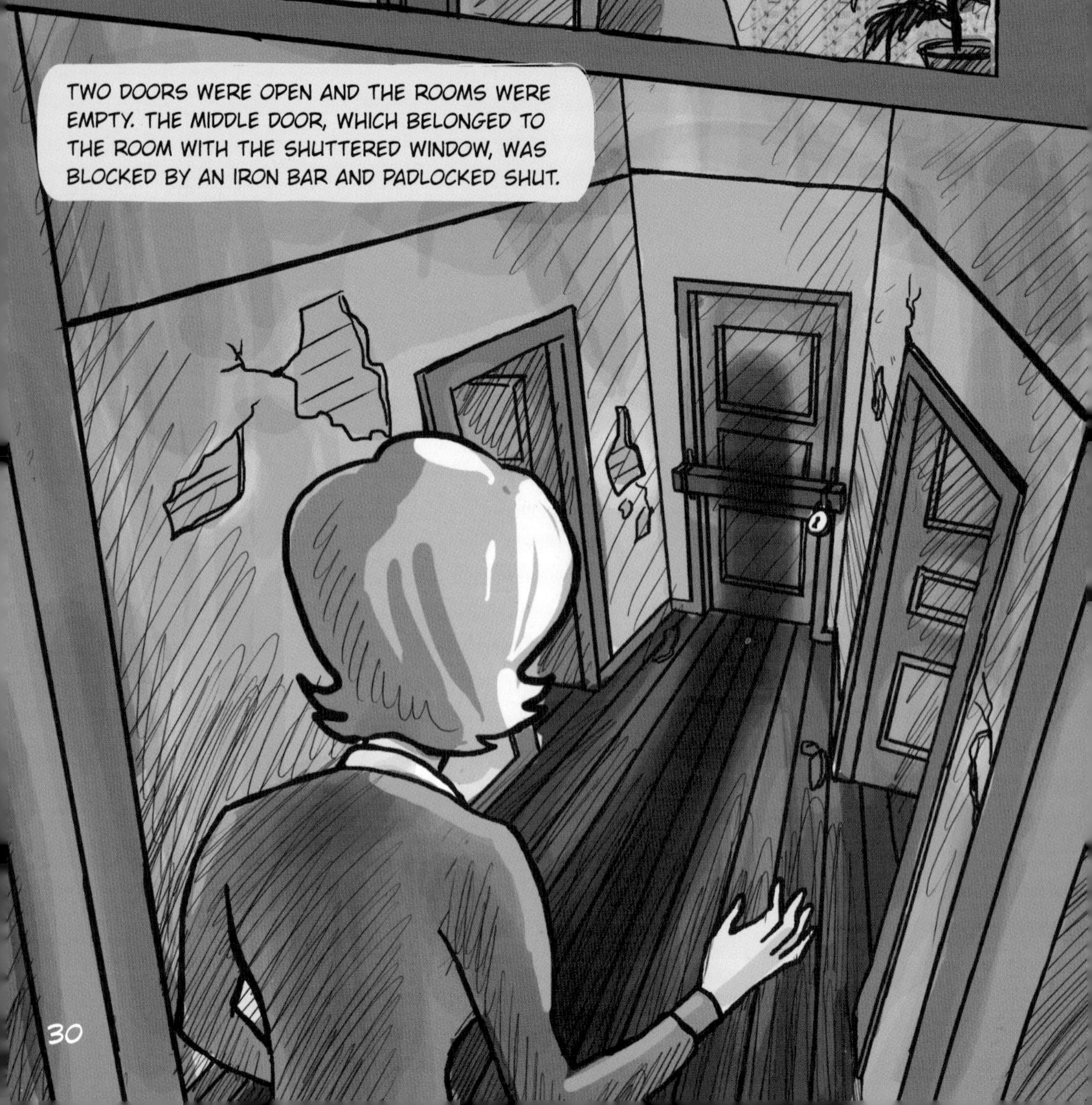
TWO DOORS WERE OPEN AND THE ROOMS WERE EMPTY. THE MIDDLE DOOR, WHICH BELONGED TO THE ROOM WITH THE SHUTTERED WINDOW, WAS BLOCKED BY AN IRON BAR AND PADLOCKED SHUT.

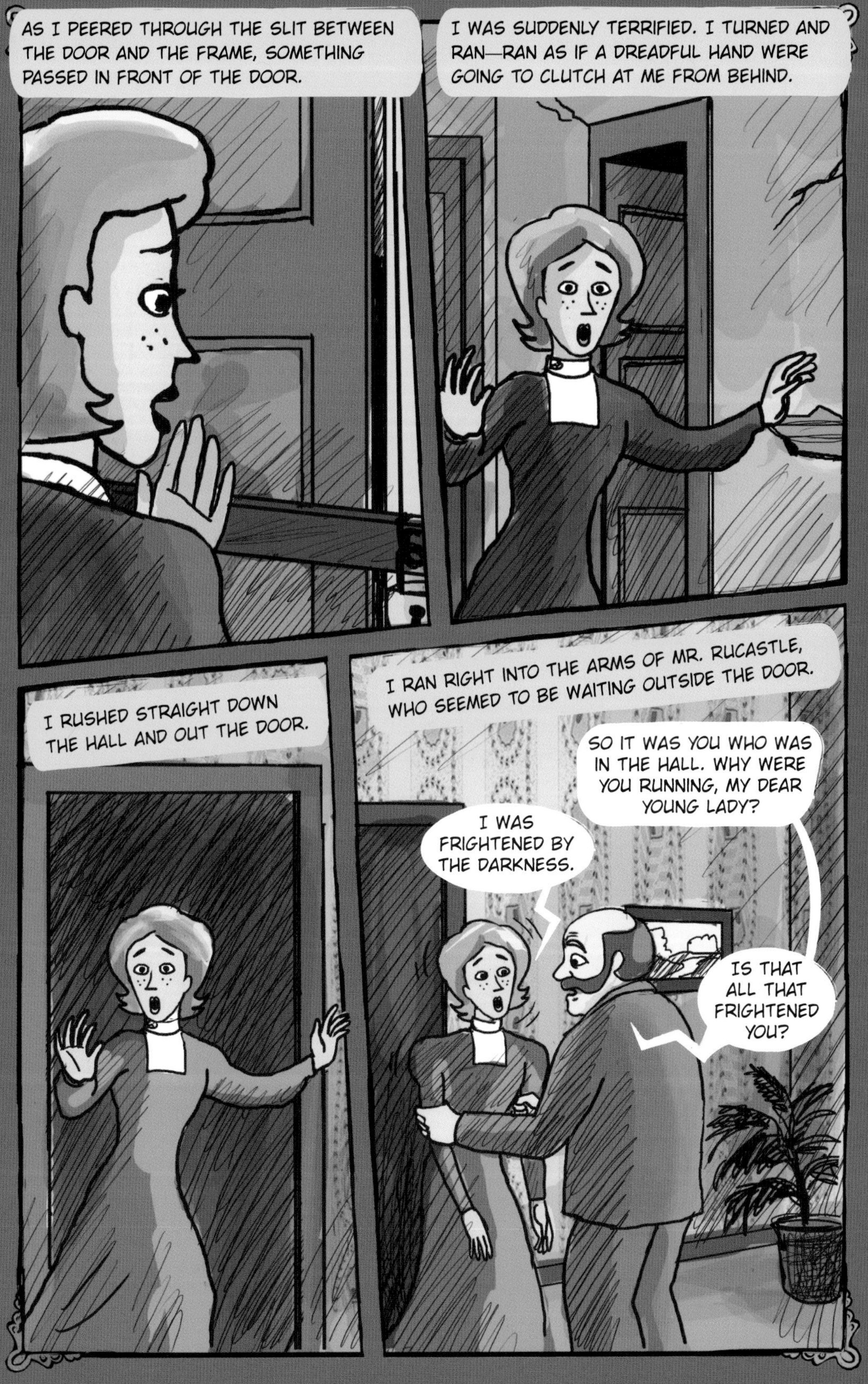

AS I PEERED THROUGH THE SLIT BETWEEN THE DOOR AND THE FRAME, SOMETHING PASSED IN FRONT OF THE DOOR.
I WAS SUDDENLY TERRIFIED. I TURNED AND RAN—RAN AS IF A DREADFUL HAND WERE GOING TO CLUTCH AT ME FROM BEHIND.
I RUSHED STRAIGHT DOWN THE HALL AND OUT THE DOOR.
I RAN RIGHT INTO THE ARMS OF MR. RUCASTLE, WHO SEEMED TO BE WAITING OUTSIDE THE DOOR.
SO IT WAS YOU WHO WAS IN THE HALL. WHY WERE YOU RUNNING, MY DEAR YOUNG LADY?
I WAS FRIGHTENED BY THE DARKNESS.
IS THAT ALL THAT FRIGHTENED YOU?

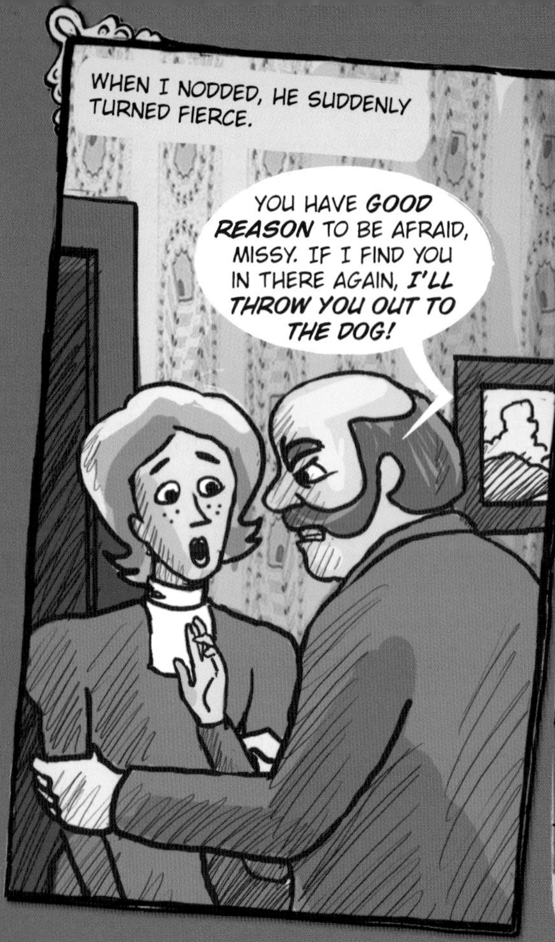
WHEN I NODDED, HE SUDDENLY TURNED FIERCE.
YOU HAVE **GOOD REASON** TO BE AFRAID, MISSY. IF I FIND YOU IN THERE AGAIN, ***I'LL THROW YOU OUT TO THE DOG!***

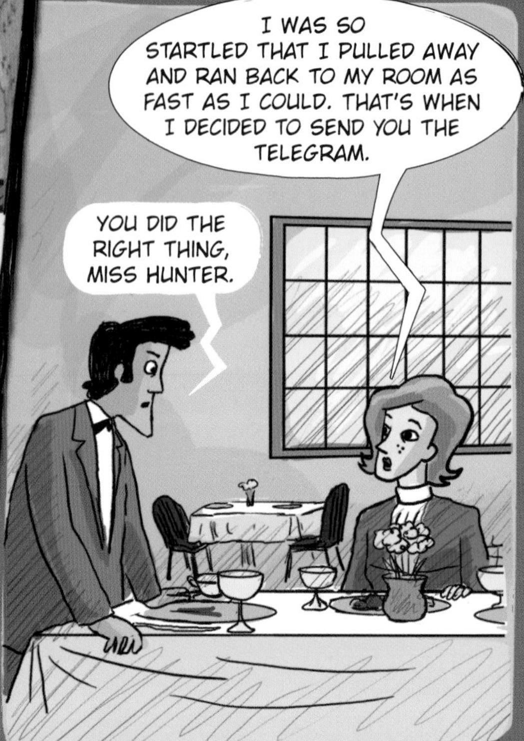
I WAS SO STARTLED THAT I PULLED AWAY AND RAN BACK TO MY ROOM AS FAST AS I COULD. THAT'S WHEN I DECIDED TO SEND YOU THE TELEGRAM.
YOU DID THE RIGHT THING, MISS HUNTER.

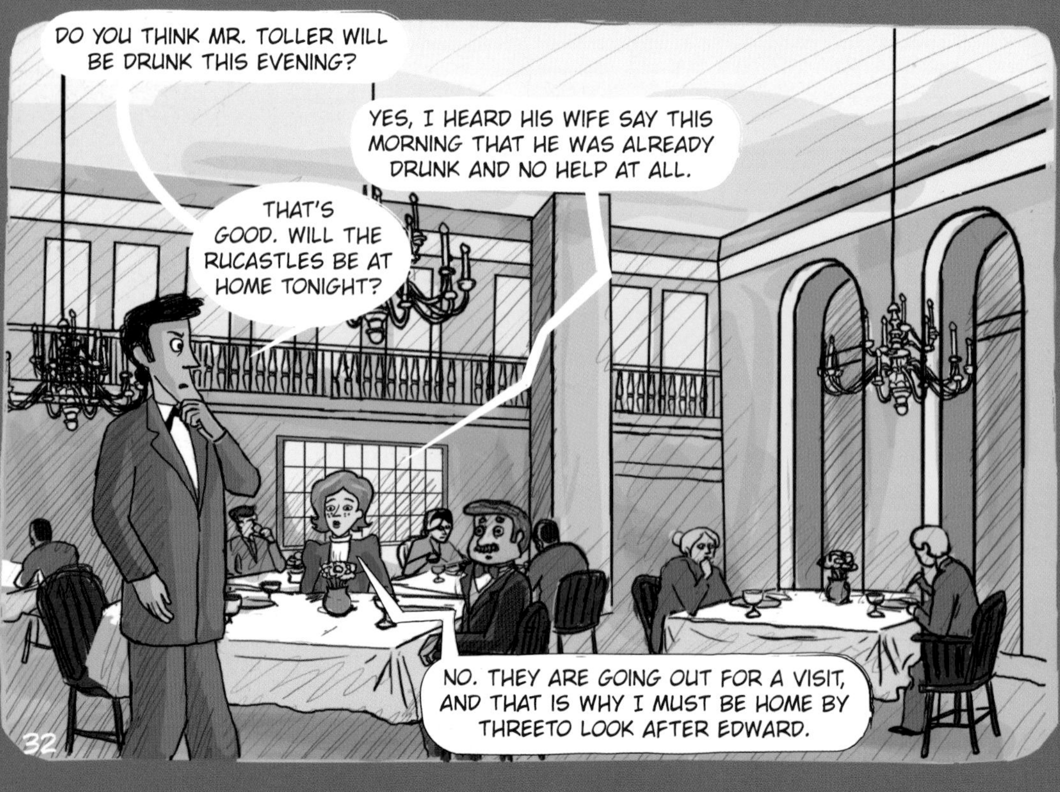
DO YOU THINK MR. TOLLER WILL BE DRUNK THIS EVENING?
YES, I HEARD HIS WIFE SAY THIS MORNING THAT HE WAS ALREADY DRUNK AND NO HELP AT ALL.
THAT'S GOOD. WILL THE RUCASTLES BE AT HOME TONIGHT?
NO. THEY ARE GOING OUT FOR A VISIT, AND THAT IS WHY I MUST BE HOME BY THREETO LOOK AFTER EDWARD.

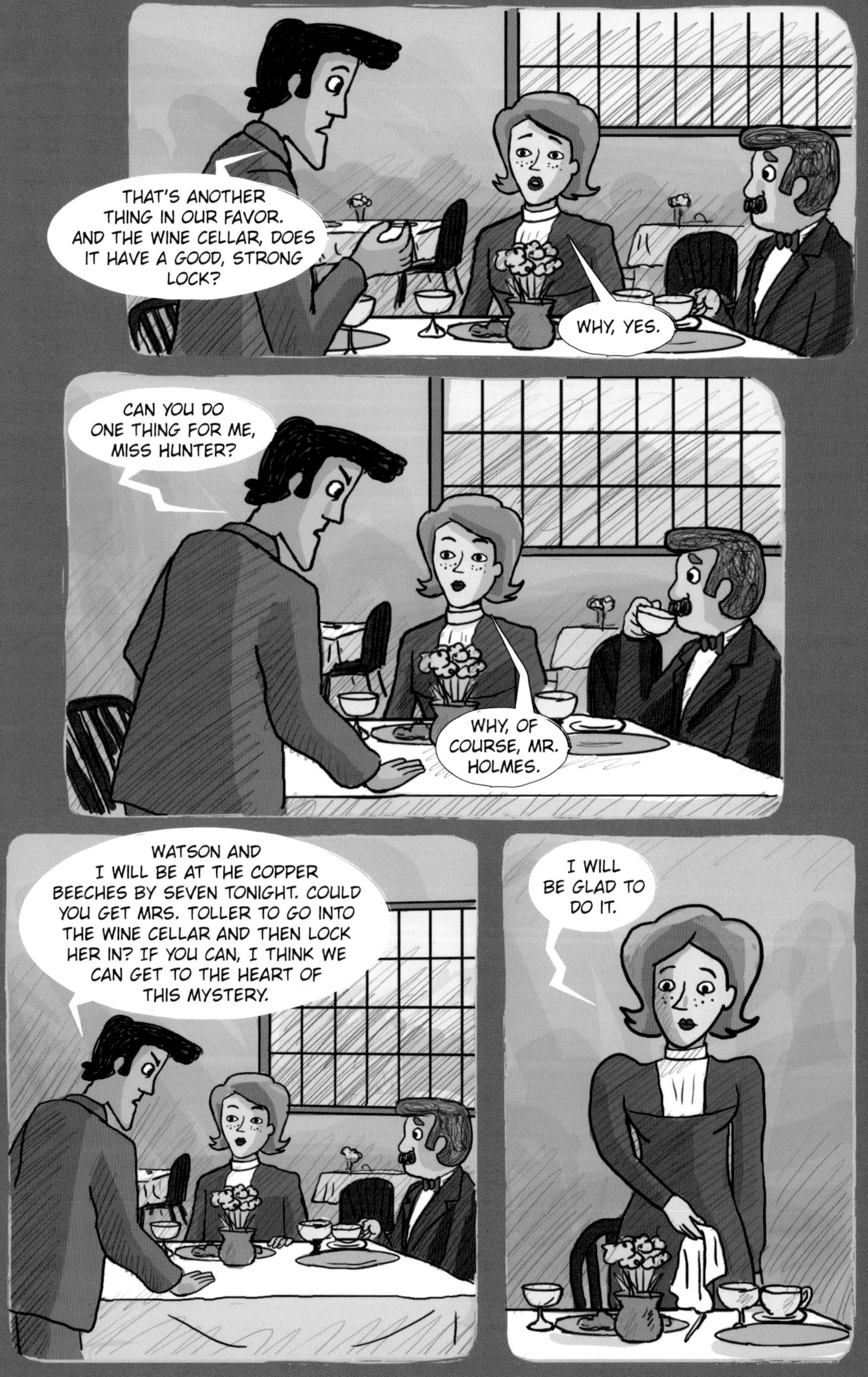
THAT'S ANOTHER THING IN OUR FAVOR. AND THE WINE CELLAR, DOES IT HAVE A GOOD, STRONG LOCK?
WHY, YES.
CAN YOU DO ONE THING FOR ME, MISS HUNTER?
WHY, OF COURSE, MR. HOLMES.
WATSON AND I WILL BE AT THE COPPER BEECHES BY SEVEN TONIGHT. COULD YOU GET MRS. TOLLER TO GO INTO THE WINE CELLAR AND THEN LOCK HER IN? IF YOU CAN, I THINK WE CAN GET TO THE HEART OF THIS MYSTERY.
I WILL BE GLAD TO DO IT.

April 27, 1894, 7:00 p.m.

We arrived at the Copper Beeches promptly at seven. The gnarled old trees, with their red leaves shining in the setting sun, marked the Rucastle home. Miss Hunter was standing on the front steps waiting for us.

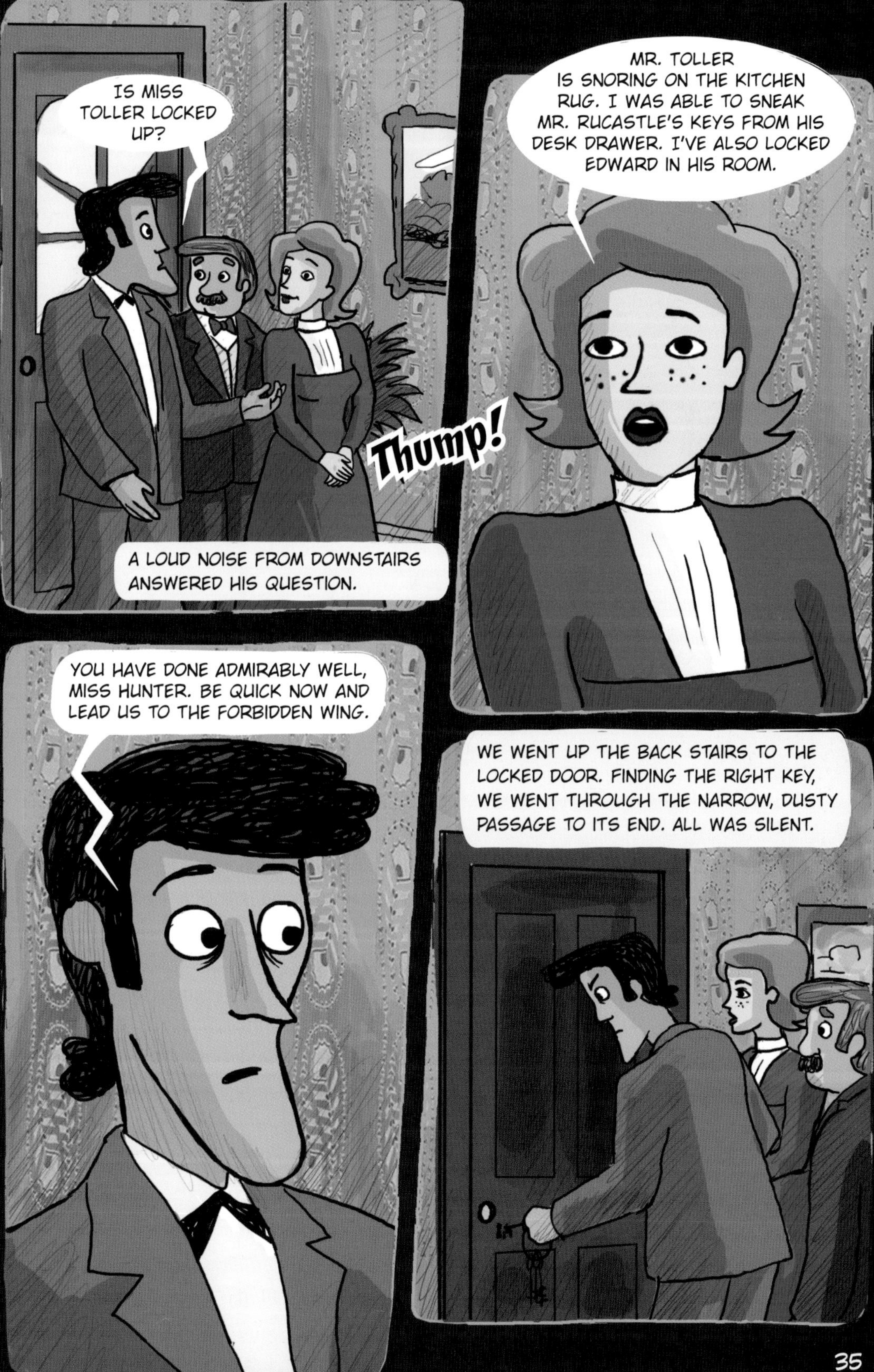
IS MISS TOLLER LOCKED UP?
A LOUD NOISE FROM DOWNSTAIRS ANSWERED HIS QUESTION.
Thump!
MR. TOLLER IS SNORING ON THE KITCHEN RUG. I WAS ABLE TO SNEAK MR. RUCASTLE'S KEYS FROM HIS DESK DRAWER. I'VE ALSO LOCKED EDWARD IN HIS ROOM.
YOU HAVE DONE ADMIRABLY WELL, MISS HUNTER. BE QUICK NOW AND LEAD US TO THE FORBIDDEN WING.
WE WENT UP THE BACK STAIRS TO THE LOCKED DOOR. FINDING THE RIGHT KEY, WE WENT THROUGH THE NARROW, DUSTY PASSAGE TO ITS END. ALL WAS SILENT.

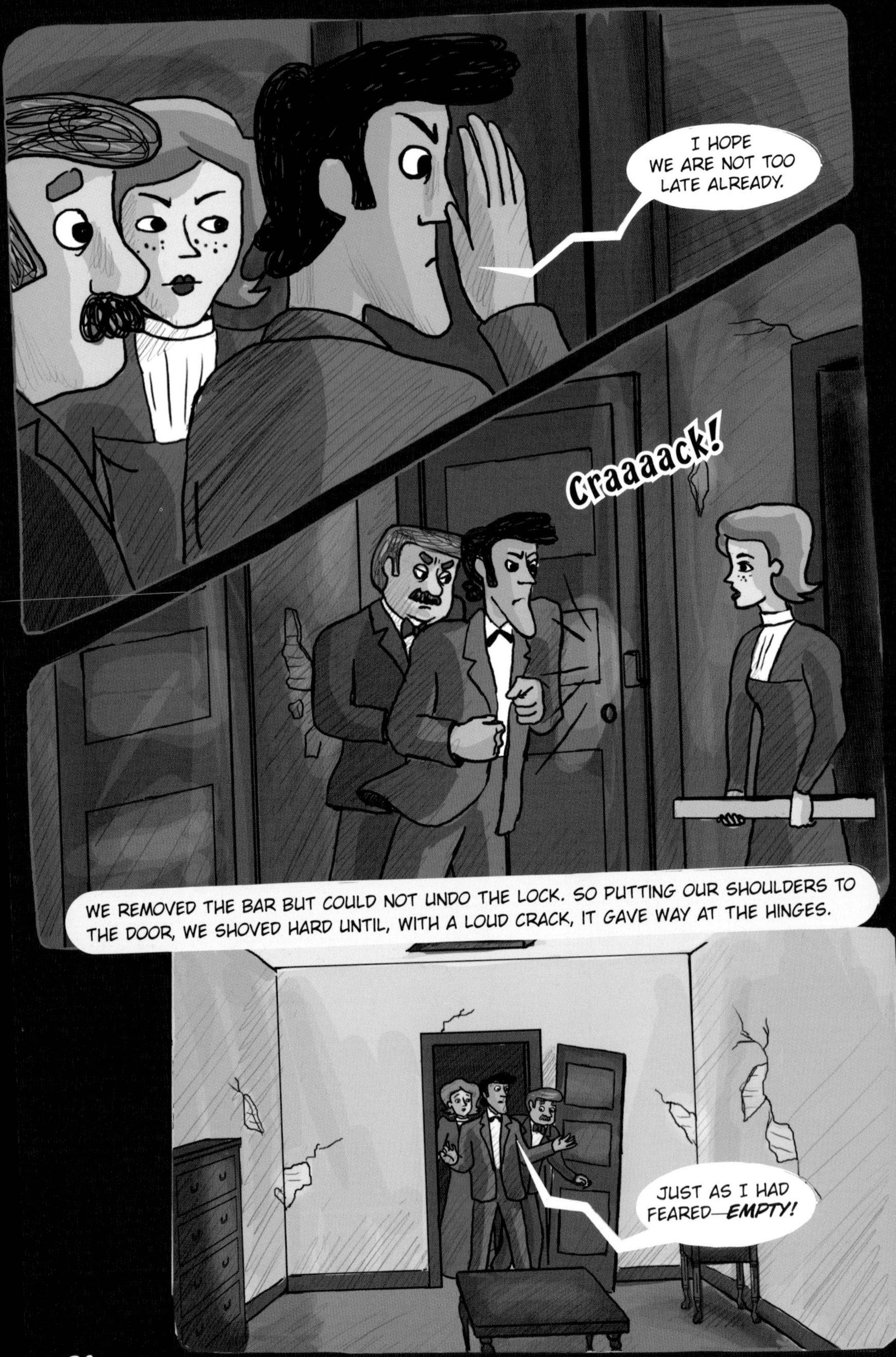
I HOPE WE ARE NOT TOO LATE ALREADY.
Craaaack!
WE REMOVED THE BAR BUT COULD NOT UNDO THE LOCK. SO PUTTING OUR SHOULDERS TO THE DOOR, WE SHOVED HARD UNTIL, WITH A LOUD CRACK, IT GAVE WAY AT THE HINGES.
JUST AS I HAD FEARED—EMPTY!

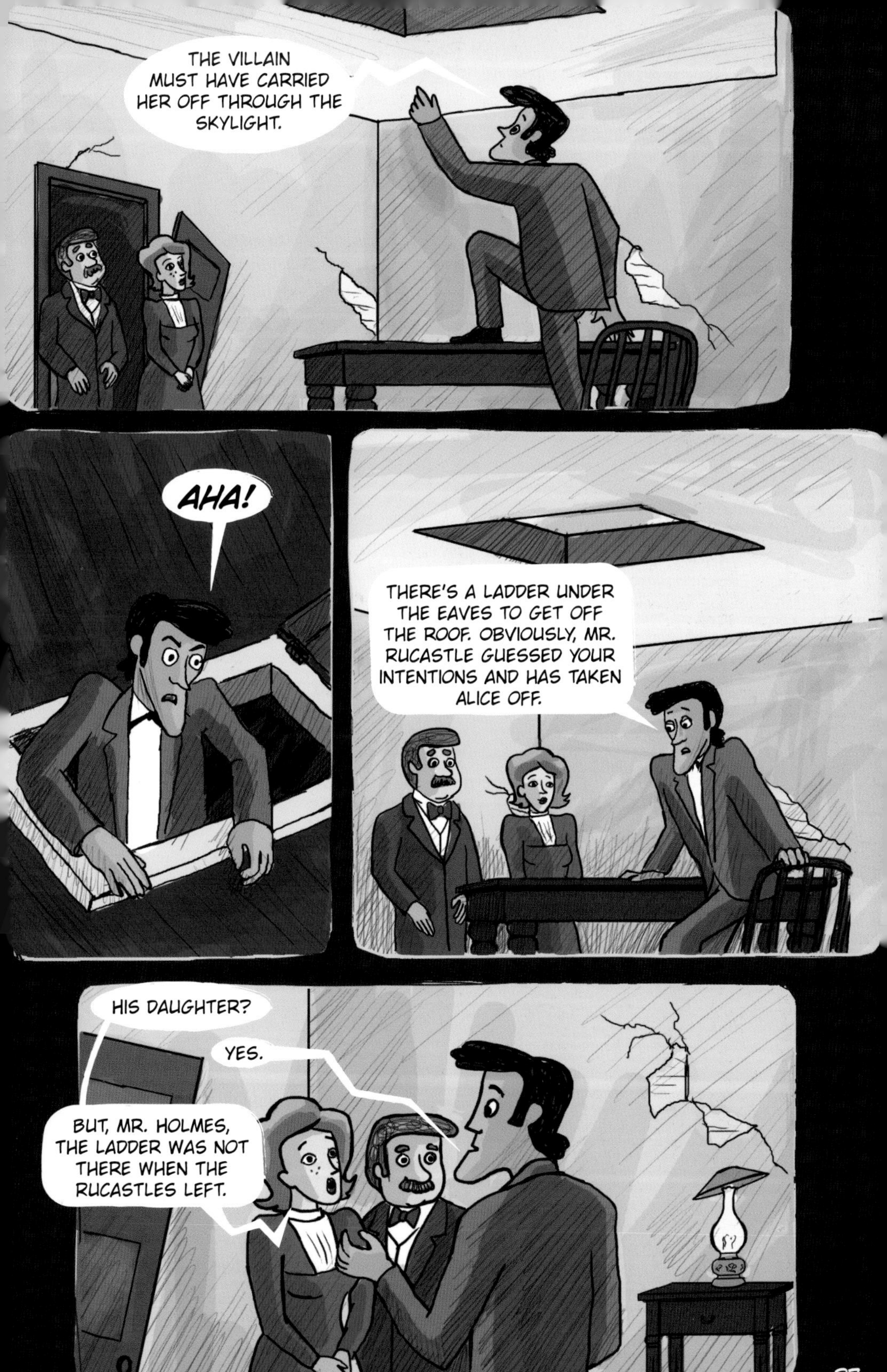
THE VILLAIN MUST HAVE CARRIED HER OFF THROUGH THE SKYLIGHT.
AHA!
THERE'S A LADDER UNDER THE EAVES TO GET OFF THE ROOF. OBVIOUSLY, MR. RUCASTLE GUESSED YOUR INTENTIONS AND HAS TAKEN ALICE OFF.
HIS DAUGHTER?
YES.
BUT, MR. HOLMES, THE LADDER WAS NOT THERE WHEN THE RUCASTLES LEFT.

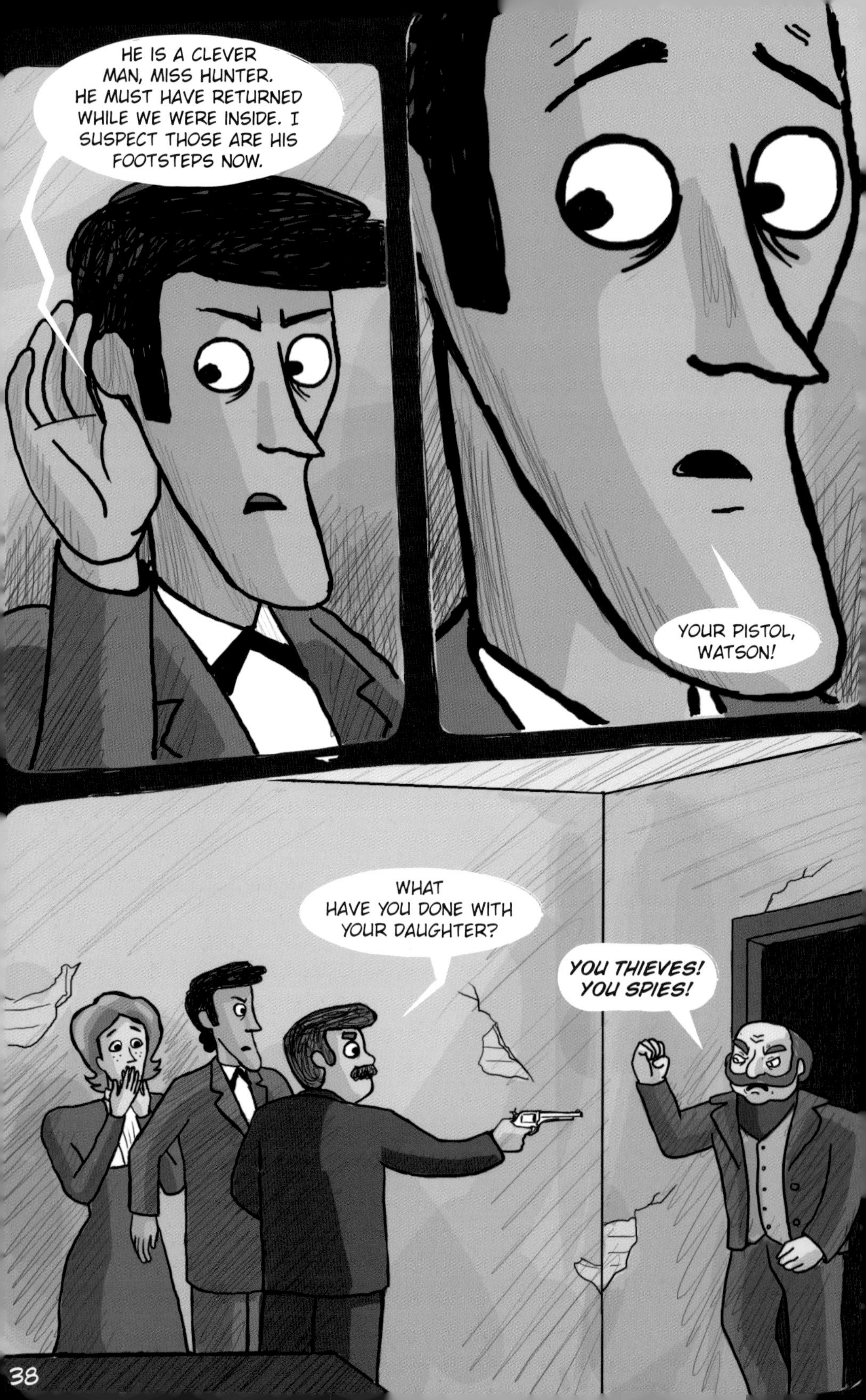
HE IS A CLEVER MAN, MISS HUNTER. HE MUST HAVE RETURNED WHILE WE WERE INSIDE. I SUSPECT THOSE ARE HIS FOOTSTEPS NOW.
YOUR PISTOL, WATSON!
WHAT HAVE YOU DONE WITH YOUR DAUGHTER?
YOU THIEVES! YOU SPIES!

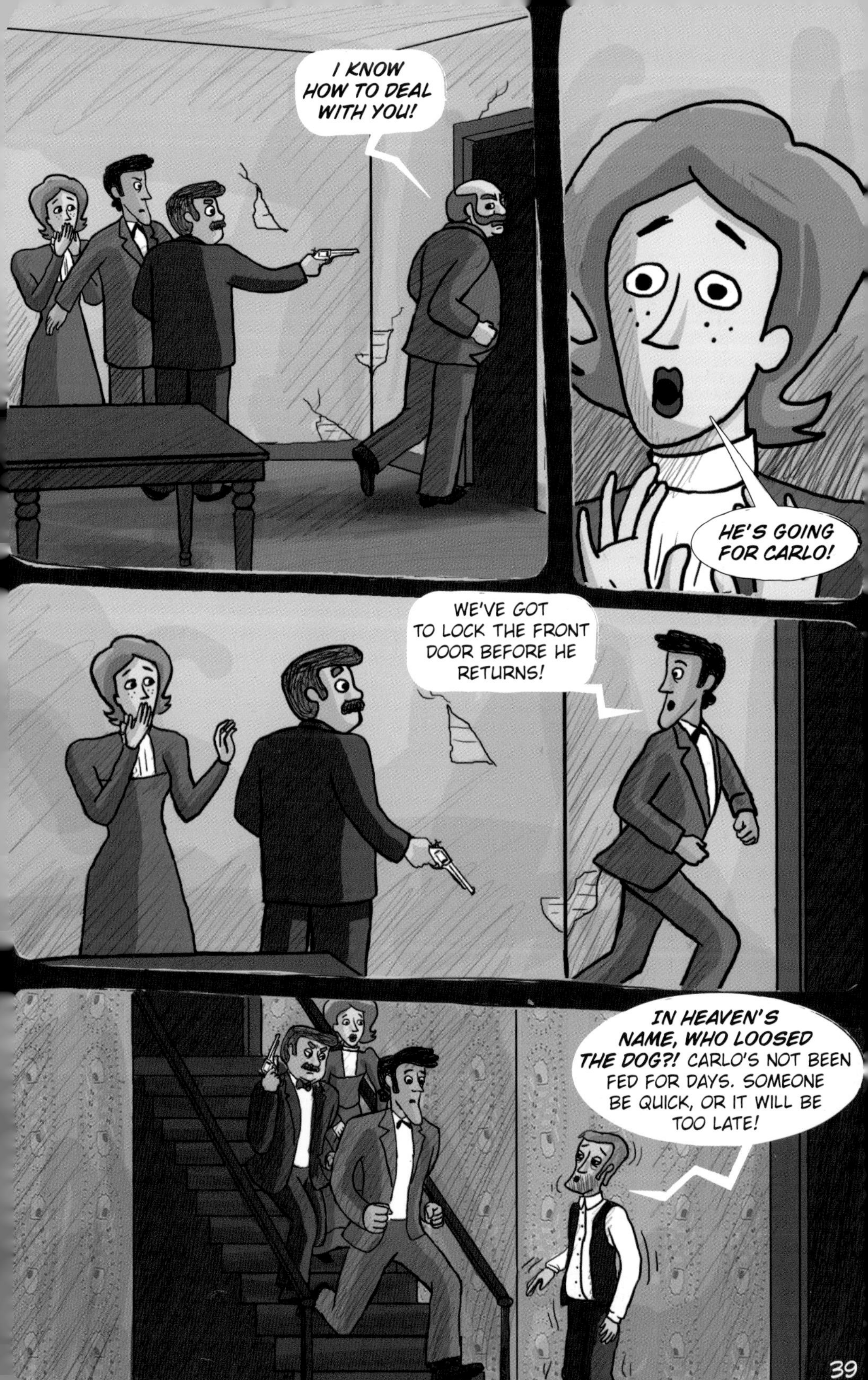
I KNOW HOW TO DEAL WITH YOU!
HE'S GOING FOR CARLO!
WE'VE GOT TO LOCK THE FRONT DOOR BEFORE HE RETURNS!
IN HEAVEN'S NAME, WHO LOOSED THE DOG?! CARLO'S NOT BEEN FED FOR DAYS. SOMEONE BE QUICK, OR IT WILL BE TOO LATE!

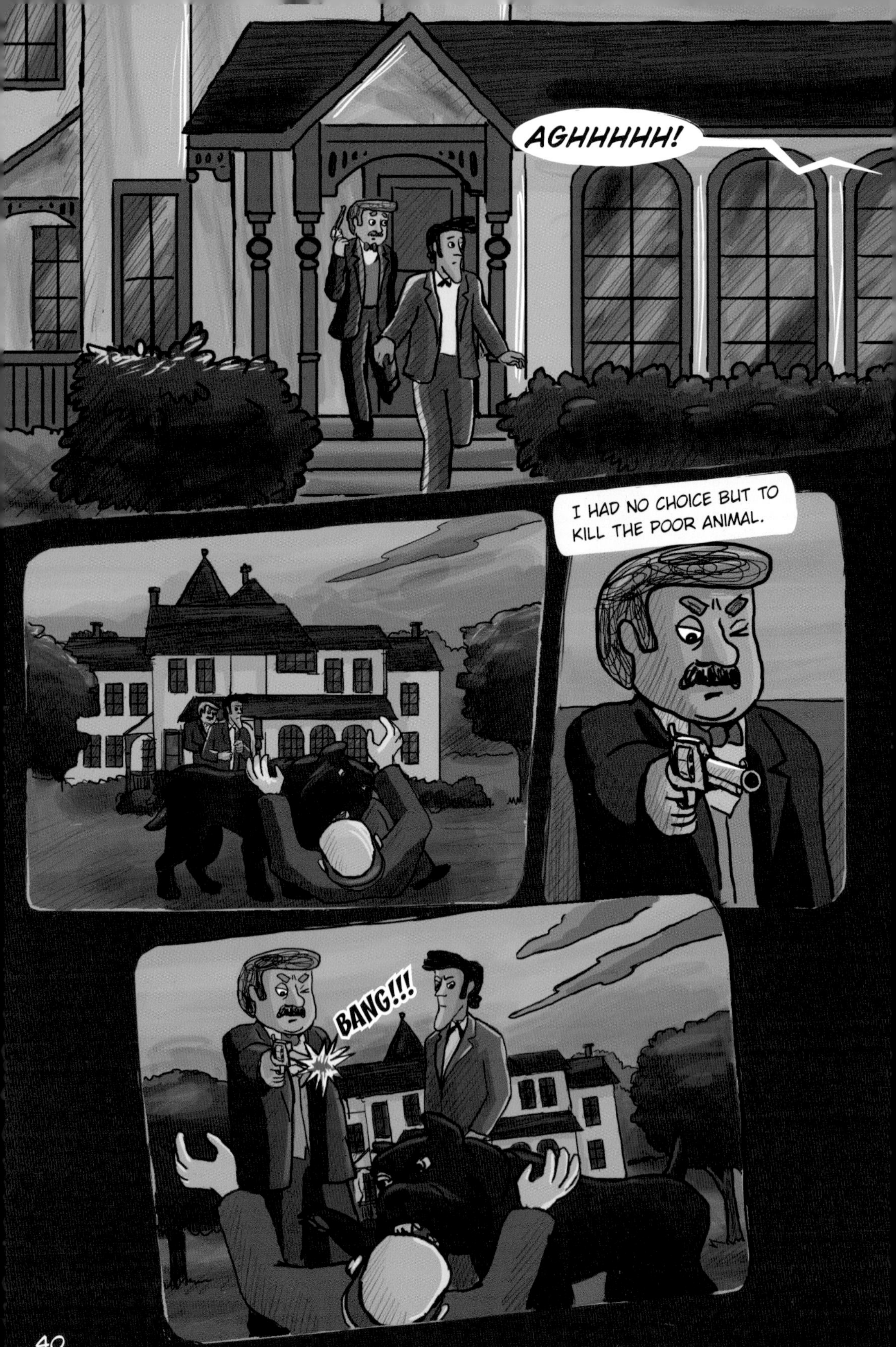
AGHHHHH!
I HAD NO CHOICE BUT TO KILL THE POOR ANIMAL.
BANG!!!

We quickly pulled the heavy animal off
Rucastle, who was mangled and losing
blood. He was barely alive as we carried him
to the house. I tended to his wounds as best I
could without my supplies. Mr. Toller went to
get the village doctor, and we let Mrs. Toller
out of the cellar.

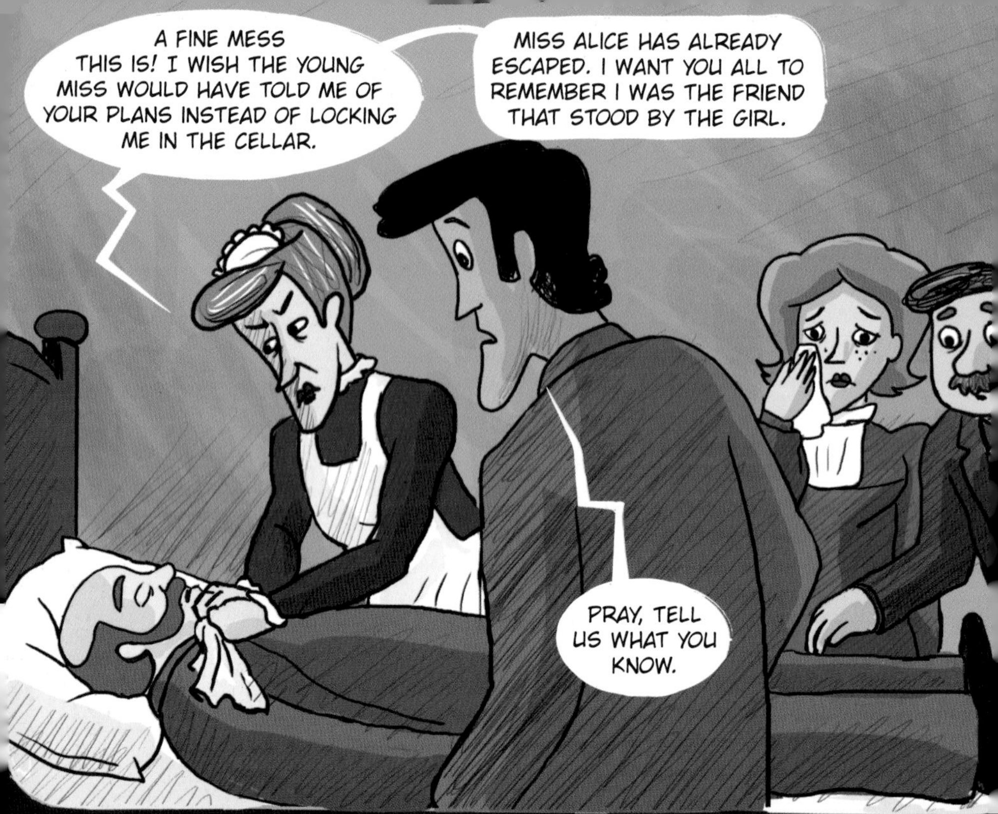
A FINE MESS THIS IS! I WISH THE YOUNG MISS WOULD HAVE TOLD ME OF YOUR PLANS INSTEAD OF LOCKING ME IN THE CELLAR.
MISS ALICE HAS ALREADY ESCAPED. I WANT YOU ALL TO REMEMBER I WAS THE FRIEND THAT STOOD BY THE GIRL.
PRAY, TELL US WHAT YOU KNOW.

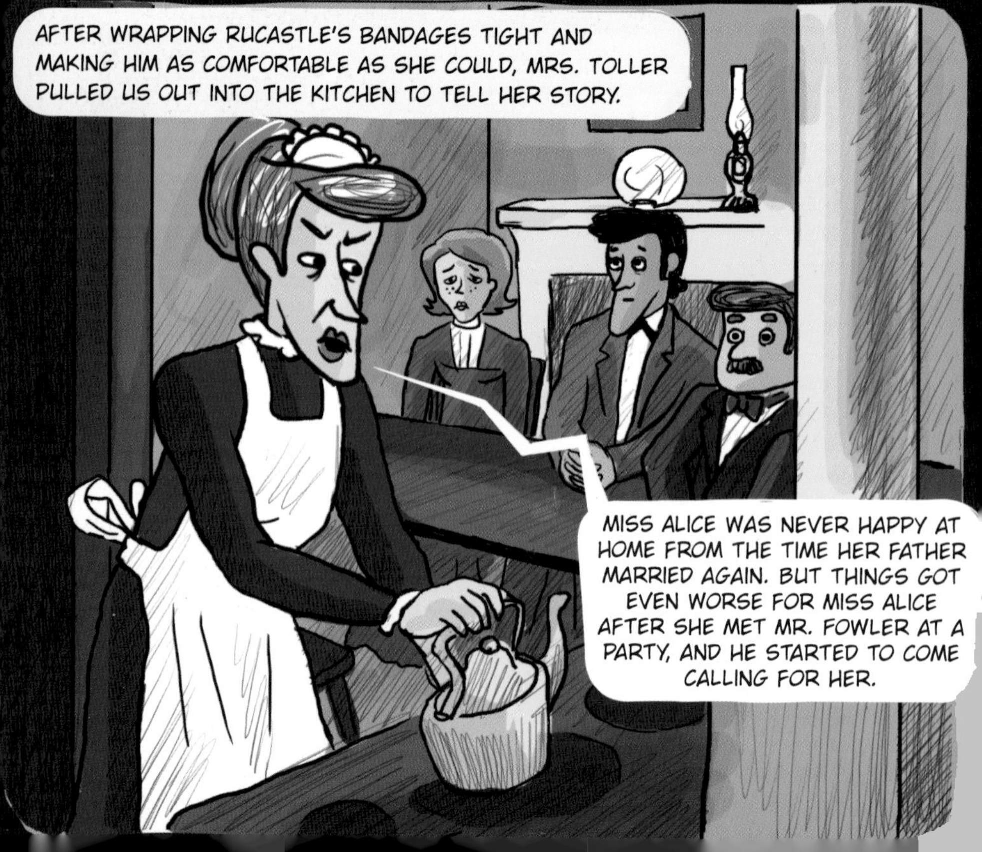
AFTER WRAPPING RUCASTLE'S BANDAGES TIGHT AND MAKING HIM AS COMFORTABLE AS SHE COULD, MRS. TOLLER PULLED US OUT INTO THE KITCHEN TO TELL HER STORY.
MISS ALICE WAS NEVER HAPPY AT HOME FROM THE TIME HER FATHER MARRIED AGAIN. BUT THINGS GOT EVEN WORSE FOR MISS ALICE AFTER SHE MET MR. FOWLER AT A PARTY, AND HE STARTED TO COME CALLING FOR HER.

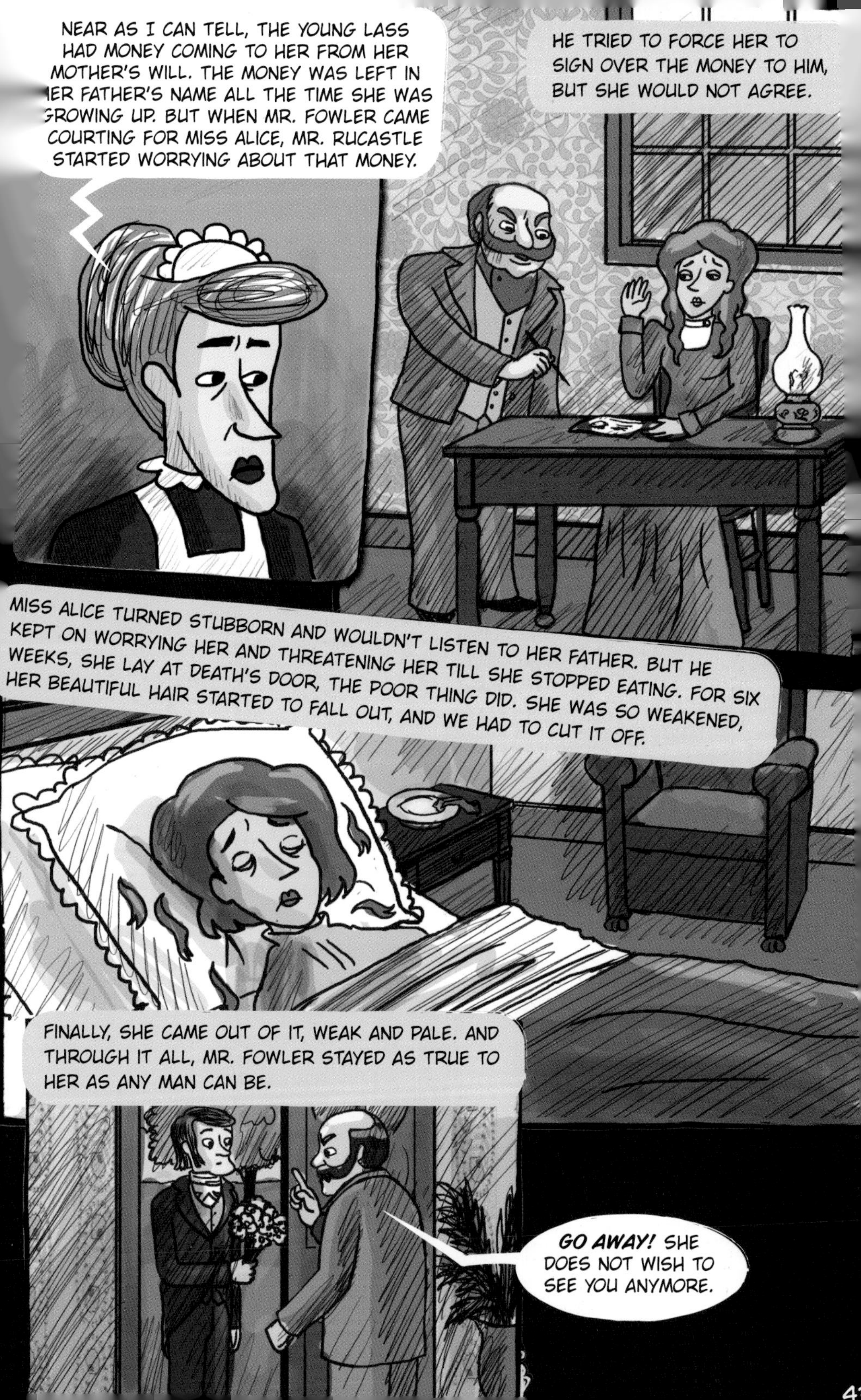

NEAR AS I CAN TELL, THE YOUNG LASS HAD MONEY COMING TO HER FROM HER MOTHER'S WILL. THE MONEY WAS LEFT IN HER FATHER'S NAME ALL THE TIME SHE WAS GROWING UP. BUT WHEN MR. FOWLER CAME COURTING FOR MISS ALICE, MR. RUCASTLE STARTED WORRYING ABOUT THAT MONEY.
HE TRIED TO FORCE HER TO SIGN OVER THE MONEY TO HIM, BUT SHE WOULD NOT AGREE.
MISS ALICE TURNED STUBBORN AND WOULDN'T LISTEN TO HER FATHER. BUT HE KEPT ON WORRYING HER AND THREATENING HER TILL SHE STOPPED EATING. FOR SIX WEEKS, SHE LAY AT DEATH'S DOOR, THE POOR THING DID. SHE WAS SO WEAKENED, HER BEAUTIFUL HAIR STARTED TO FALL OUT, AND WE HAD TO CUT IT OFF.
FINALLY, SHE CAME OUT OF IT, WEAK AND PALE. AND THROUGH IT ALL, MR. FOWLER STAYED AS TRUE TO HER AS ANY MAN CAN BE.
GO AWAY! SHE DOES NOT WISH TO SEE YOU ANYMORE.

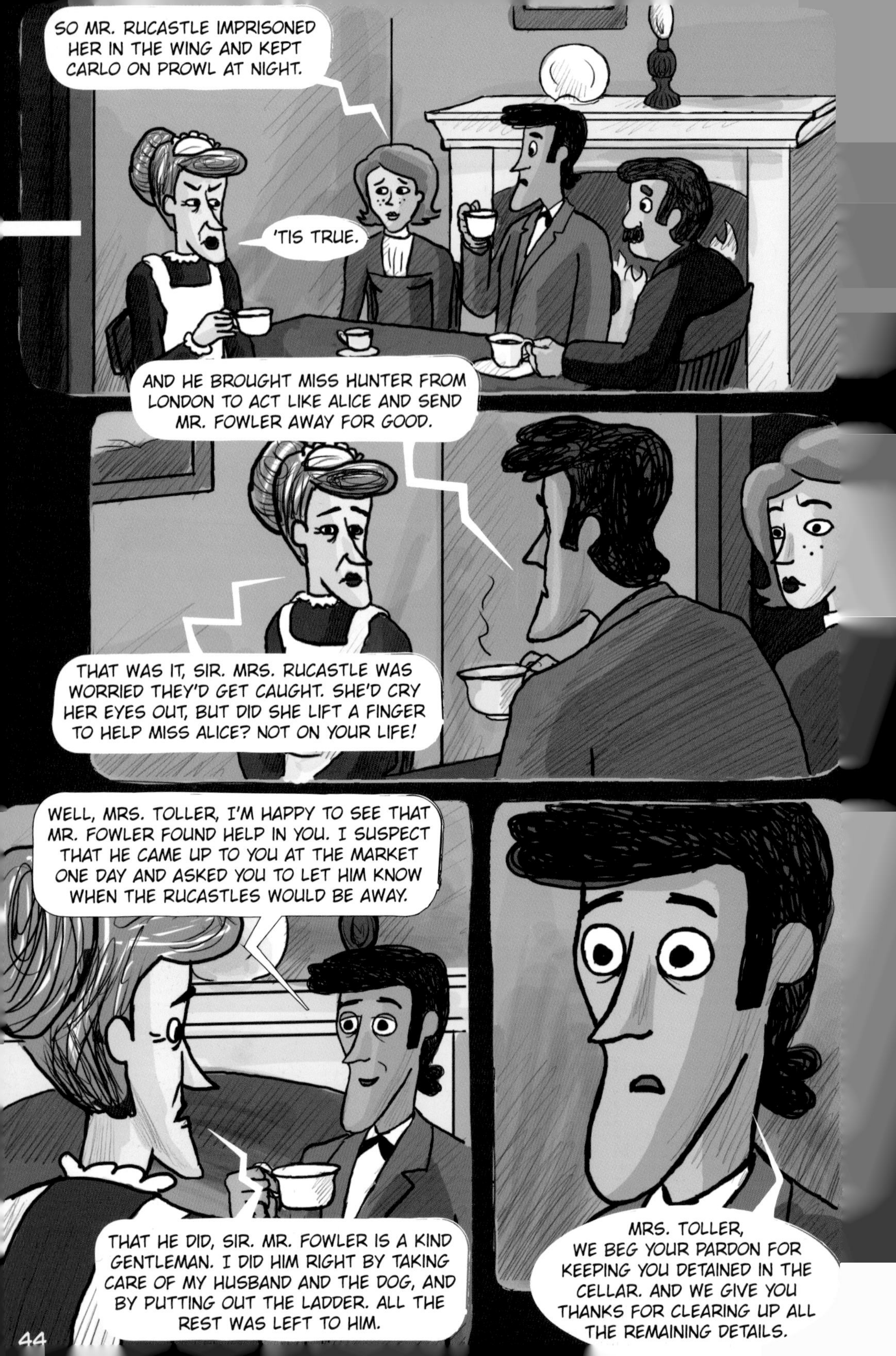
SO MR. RUCASTLE IMPRISONED HER IN THE WING AND KEPT CARLO ON PROWL AT NIGHT.
'TIS TRUE.
AND HE BROUGHT MISS HUNTER FROM LONDON TO ACT LIKE ALICE AND SEND MR. FOWLER AWAY FOR GOOD.
THAT WAS IT, SIR. MRS. RUCASTLE WAS WORRIED THEY'D GET CAUGHT. SHE'D CRY HER EYES OUT, BUT DID SHE LIFT A FINGER TO HELP MISS ALICE? NOT ON YOUR LIFE!
WELL, MRS. TOLLER, I'M HAPPY TO SEE THAT MR. FOWLER FOUND HELP IN YOU. I SUSPECT THAT HE CAME UP TO YOU AT THE MARKET ONE DAY AND ASKED YOU TO LET HIM KNOW WHEN THE RUCASTLES WOULD BE AWAY.
THAT HE DID, SIR. MR. FOWLER IS A KIND GENTLEMAN. I DID HIM RIGHT BY TAKING CARE OF MY HUSBAND AND THE DOG, AND BY PUTTING OUT THE LADDER. ALL THE REST WAS LEFT TO HIM.
MRS. TOLLER, WE BEG YOUR PARDON FOR KEEPING YOU DETAINED IN THE CELLAR. AND WE GIVE YOU THANKS FOR CLEARING UP ALL THE REMAINING DETAILS.

J ust then the doctor arrived. Some friends delivered Mrs. Rucastle home. Holmes and I led Miss Hunter out of the house to spare her further distress.

Later, we heard that Mr. Rucastle survived the accident but was a broken man, needing constant nursing by his wife. Edward was sent to a new school where he learned to be a kinder child. Alice and Jason Fowler married and settled down to live in a nearby village. As for Violet Hunter, she eventually formed her own boarding school, where she met with great success. And thus ended the unusual story of the Copper Beeches.

From the Desk of
John H. Watson, M.D.

The Adventure at the Copper Beeches: How Did Holmes Solve It?

What clues made Holmes suspicious of Mr. Rucastle?

Mr. Rucastle's decision to hire Miss Hunter based only on her appearance made Holmes suspicious. Since Mr. Rucastle was also willing to pay Miss Hunter so much above the normal wage, Holmes became even more concerned.

Holmes was also disturbed by the cruel play of Mr. Rucastle's child. Holmes had often noticed that you could tell quite a bit about parents by looking at their children. Another clue to Mr. Rucastle's true nature was his treatment of the dog—his cruel starving of the animal to make it vicious.

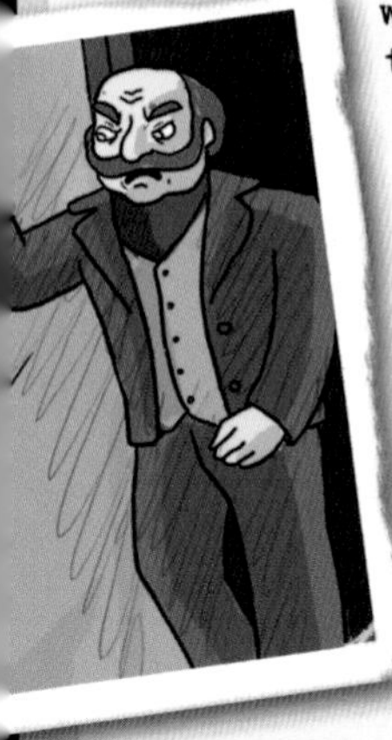

Why did Holmes suspect that Miss Hunter was hired to impersonate Alice?

Since Mr. Rucastle asked Miss Hunter to cut off her hair, wear a worn blue dress, and sit by the windows, Holmes figured that Mr. Rucastle wanted her to look like someone else. This was confirmed when Miss Hunter said that she had found a coil of hair that looked just like her own. Holmes suspected that it had once belonged to the woman she was imitating. Who was this woman? She had to be someone who had once lived in the house—and that could only be Alice Rucastle.

How did Holmes conclude that someone outside the family was involved in the mystery?

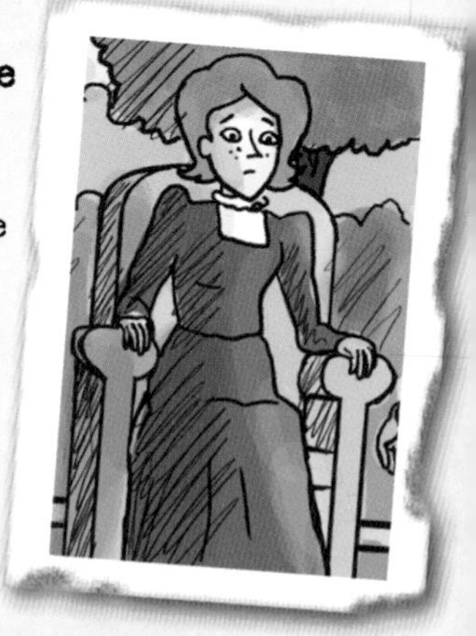

Because Miss Hunter had to wear the dress in front of the windows, Holmes was sure that the performance was done so someone outside the house could see it. The young man was the next clue. Holmes assumed that the stranger on the front road was Alice's friend. Holmes also figured that Mr. Rucastle had Carlo put out at night to keep this man away from his daughter.

How did Holmes conclude that money was involved?

The final questions were: Why did the Rucastles want to pretend that Alice was still living there? Had they killed her? Had they sent her away? Holmes suspected that the answers to these questions were to be found in the forbidden wing. He thought it was likely that the Rucastles were holding Alice hostage in the wing and that they were doing it for money. Mrs. Toller's explanation of Alice's inheritance confirmed this theory.

Further Reading and Websites

Barnett, Mac. *The Case of the Case of Mistaken Identity.* New York: Simon & Schuster, 2008.

Crosby, Jeff. *Little Lions, Bull Baiters, & Hunting Hounds: A History of Dog Breeds.* New York: Tundra Books, 2008.

Haddix, Margaret Peterson. *Double Identity.* New York: Simon & Schuster, 2007.

Landau, Elaine. *Mastiffs Are the Best!* Minneapolis: Lerner Publications Company, 2011.

MacDonald, Fiona. *You Wouldn't Want To be a Victorian Servant!: A Thankless Job You'd Rather Not Have.* Danbury, CT: Franklin Watts, 2007.

Sherlock Holmes Museum
http://www.sherlock-holmes.co.uk

Stolarz, Laurie Faria. *Deadly Little Secret.* New York: Hyperion, 2008.

221 Baker Street
http://221bakerstreet.org

About the Author

Sir Arthur Conan Doyle was born on May 22, 1859. He became a doctor in 1882. When this career did not prove successful, Doyle started writing stories. In addition to the popular Sherlock Holmes short stories and novels, Doyle also wrote historical novels, romances, and plays.

About the Adapters

Murray Shaw's lifelong passion for Sherlock Holmes began when he was a child. He was the author of the Match Wits with Sherlock Holmes series published in the 1990s. For decades, he was a popular speaker in public schools and libraries on the adventures of Holmes and Watson.

M. J. Cosson is the author of more than fifty books, both fiction and nonfiction, for children and young adults. She has long been a fan of mysteries and especially of the great detective, Sherlock Holmes. In fact, she has participated in the production of several Sherlock Holmes plays. A native of Iowa, Cosson lives in the Texas Hill Country with her husband, dogs, and cat.

About the Illustrators

Sophie Rohrbach began her career after graduating in display design at the Chambre des Commerce in France. She went on to design displays in many top department stores including Galerias Lafayette. She also studied illustration at Emile Cohl school in Lyon, France, where she now lives with her daughter. Rohrbach has illustrated many children's books. She is passionate about the colors and patterns that she uses in her illustrations.

JT Morrow has worked as a freelance illustrator for over twenty years and has won several awards. He specializes in doing parodies and imitations of the Old and Modern Masters—everyone from da Vinci to Picasso. JT also exhibits his paintings at galleries near his home. He lives just south of San Francisco with his wife and daughter.